LIKE A BAD MEMORY

A Novel

JIM WOODS

ACKNOWLEDGMENTS

I would like to thank each of these people for so many reasons: Spencer DeVeau, Sarah Lamb, Anna McKenzie, John Bucher, Todd Foley, Katelyn Johnson, Chris Morris, Gary Ware, Tammy Helfrich, Kent Sanders, and Melissa Reagan. This book is here because of you!

I want to thank these amazing people who were extremely supportive and encouraging as I wrote this book: Duane Carothers, Sheila Galeano, Andrew Hagen, Shawn Hartoog, Shane Kardos, Nicholas Kardos, Vincent Marchetti, Aaron Ridenbaugh, and Mark Whitmore.

Thanks to Jeremy Banzhof and Chrysti Inden for their valuable insights.

Thanks to Carmen DeVeau for all of your help with the book covers.

Special thanks to Kristal, Kate, and Jack. I love you very much.

"If you're going through hell, keep going."

—Winston Churchill

Sergeant Ryan Malone took a deep breath and steadied himself as he tightened his grasp on his gun. He wasn't sure he could get up from the ground. He focused his thoughts on his surroundings to help block out the distraction. He was alone now. Just a few feet in front of him was the dead body of Peewee, an enforcer for the Gangster Disciples. Behind him was a young Gangster Disciple named Shorty. Shorty squealed in pain after Malone shot him in the kneecap.

Malone tried to get up to his feet and immediately fell back down. He tried again and slowly got back up. On the other side of the Navy Pier parking deck, Alex Ramirez, another member of the Gang Task Force, had been shot. Malone started limping toward him when he heard an SUV's engine start. Tires squealed as it rounded a corner toward the exit. Antoine, leader of the Gangster Disciples, was trying to get away. It was close. Malone stepped into the vehicle's path, firing at the windshield. The SUV swerved, lost control, and smashed into a concrete column.

Malone limped toward the vehicle as smoke rose from under the hood. He could see that Antoine was still in the driver's seat. Malone pulled a clip out of his vest and reloaded his gun. He carefully approached the SUV. "Freeze! Put your fucking hands up!"

Through the window he saw Antoine's face was bloody, and he wasn't moving. Malone kept his gun aimed for a few more seconds. Still no movement.

Suddenly, Antoine opened his eyes and fired a burst from his Glock, hitting Malone in the chest and knocking him to the ground.

Antoine tumbled out of the driver's side and limped away. Malone leaned forward and steadied himself on the SUV as he stood up.

Antoine had collapsed on his way to the exit and got back up. As he ran, Malone aimed his gun and said, "Freeze! Drop it, asshole. It's over."

Malone watched as Antoine tucked the Glock into the front of his pants and held his hands up over his head. "No, it ain't, motherfucker," he said. "Not even close. You ain't gonna win, you dumb fuck. You're never gonna—"

Antoine put his arms down and spun around with the Glock drawn in his right hand. Malone fired a shot into Antoine's forehead and watched his body fall to the ground.

"Why don't you shut the fuck up?" Malone coughed and started to spit up blood. He slipped his hand underneath his body armor. Blood covered his fingertips. After several wobbly steps, he collapsed on the ground.

Thoughts started to drift and the images of everyone he'd lost jumbled together in his mind.

His partner Max.

Fellow officers Johnny and Leo.

Mikey, his informant.

His nephew Andrew.

Malone laid on the ground as blood slowly pooled around

him. He looked upward and saw Ramirez crouched over him. "I thought you were a goner."

"Naw. Vest caught it. I'll be sore as hell later, but I'm still here."

"Good," Malone said. He shut his eyes as the sound of sirens swelled in the night.

CHAPTER 1

Malone thought he was dead. Instead, he found himself in a small room and stuck in an uncomfortable hospital bed at Mercy Hospital. After two surgeries for multiple gunshot wounds to the chest, a skin graft for third-degree burns on his right arm, and four weeks of physical therapy, Malone had a lot of time to think. During his stint in the hospital, he felt like shit but had managed to stop drinking.

Once he got out, he tried to move back in with Ann, but she told him she wanted to take things slowly. Malone didn't blame her. He lost track trying to remember how many times he'd told her in the past that he'd stopped drinking. But this time, he was determined to stay sober. If he didn't, he knew Ann would never let him see their son James.

Malone tried to distract himself by watching television, but that only lasted for about a day and a half. No matter what he did, his mind raced and he couldn't stop thinking about what happened to the other members of the Gang Task Force. His partner Max was shot and killed. Leo and Johnny were also both shot and killed. The shooter, Ace, had been in the wind for close to six weeks now. Something about the whole situation didn't sit right with Malone. Either it was total incompetence by CPD or there was more to the story.

Now all there was for Malone to do was the work. Police reports, photos, and other documents covered his apartment. Stacks of notes littered every surface. He spent hours going over case file after case file, trying to sort out everything that had happened.

At this point, Malone had more questions than ever and few answers. He went back to what he knew for sure: the former leader of the Gangster Disciples, Antoine, was dead, and it would only be a matter of time until someone took his place. Before Antoine died, he said something about having a fentanyl lab, but Malone knew that could have been bullshit coming from a known bullshitter. The Latin Kings and either the Sinaloa Cartel or the Jalisco New Generation Cartel were part of the mix as well.

His eyes were bleary and his mind was spent from hours of staring at documents. He needed a distraction. Malone paced around his apartment, gazed out the window, listened to the radio, and brainlessly watched TV. Maybe that was part of why he drank: it made him crash harder. Now that he wasn't drinking, he was lucky to get a few hours of sleep a night.

Malone wandered into the kitchen and stood in front of the sink. He rubbed his palms on his face and then looked at the amber colored prescription bottle. He opened it and held the last four oxycodone pills in his hand. Staring at them, he thought about gulping all of them down, but tightened his jaw. A scowl formed on his face. He yanked the pantry door open and dropped the pills into the white trashcan. Two pills fell into some coffee grounds. The other two plopped into a white Chinese food takeout carton and sat on a bed of uneaten chow mein noodles.

No more. He was done. He had to stay sharp. Malone

rubbed the palms of his hands on his face once more and got a drink of water.

Back at the couch, he stared down at the files he had scattered all over the coffee table. One was a bloody photo of Antoine lying dead on the ground. Another photo showed a dead man inside the back of a white van. He studied the van, then turned his attention to the figure inside. This man looked somewhat familiar.

Malone shuffled through the photos again. He was sure that he'd seen that prick before, but couldn't place him. He was young, Black, and had a shaved head and goatee. No visible tattoos. Malone exhaled as he stared at the photo. Maybe he'd arrested him once? He couldn't remember. Everything was blurring together. He needed to go back to sleep. Even if only for an hour.

He dropped the photos on the coffee table and laid down on the couch. As he started to doze off, his phone rang. Ann's name flashed on the screen. After a deep breath, Malone answered.

"Hey. So, I guess you're heading back to work today, right? How're you feeling?" Ann asked.

Malone yawned quietly and tried to ignore the headache that reminded him of a hangover.

"Hey. I—uh—I'm pretty good. Just about to shower and get ready."

"Can we bring you breakfast? James has been begging to see you."

"Yeah. That sounds better than a granola bar or Pop-Tart."

"Good. We'll see you in a few minutes."

The call disconnected, and Malone glanced around. He couldn't let them see the place like this. He scooped up the police reports, photos, notepads, and files covering the floor and coffee table. Malone crammed all the paperwork into three battered filing boxes. Next were the fast food wrappers, dirty socks, pants, and a shirt. He hurried to the kitchen and moved a couple pizza boxes from the countertop to the trashcan and placed a stack of dirty dishes in the sink. Glancing down at himself, he went to his bedroom and pulled on a black t-shirt and a pair of shorts, just as there was a knock on the door.

When he opened it, James ran into the room.

"Look what I got, Dad!" James said as he held up a white bakery bag.

"Did you get some donuts?"

"Uh-huh!"

Ann slowly followed James into Malone's apartment and set the newspaper on the kitchen counter.

"Donuts, huh?" Malone said in surprise.

"He begged and begged for them." Ann shrugged her shoulders and smiled.

"I see. I just started some coffee. Want some?"

"Yeah, I guess that'd be fine."

Malone noticed Ann's voice was a bit off. Quieter and without any emotion.

"Can I watch TV, Dad?"

"Sure, buddy."

James ran over to the couch and turned on the television with the remote.

"You okay?" Malone asked quietly, as he got two cheap white coffee mugs from the cabinet.

"No. I'm not. James came running into my room crying in the middle of the night. Police sirens woke him up."

"What happened?"

"I'm not sure. I talked to Linda a few houses down and she said she thought she heard some gunshots."

"I see," Malone said as he grabbed some creamer out of the refrigerator.

"Seems like things are only getting worse..." Ann couldn't finish the sentence.

Malone put his hand on her shoulder. "Yeah, I know. But "Look, I gotta believe I can help make things better. That's why I became a cop. I'm not a guy who gives up on anything easily. Ever."

Ann turned around and looked Malone in the eyes. "I know. And that's what scares me." Ann said. The coffee pot started to sputter and Ann flinched.

"It's okay." Malone gave her a grin. "I know this silly thing is pretty loud."

"Yeah, it sure is."

"Could serve as a backup alarm, right?" Malone joked as he filled the first mug and carefully gave it to Ann. As he poured his cup, he noticed a small chip on the mug lip. He turned the mug as he followed Ann to the couch.

Malone sat down and put his arm around James. "You save any for us, or did ya eat 'em all?"

"*Maybe*," James grinned slyly.

Malone peeked inside the white bag. There were still four donuts left. He pulled out a powdered donut and took a big bite. It was good, but almost too sweet. He washed it down with some coffee. "You working today?" Malone asked as he glanced at the headlines on the front page of the *Chicago Sun-Times*.

"Yeah, I'm going into the office today. I can keep an eye out for some houses in nice areas."

Malone scowled, but covered it with the coffee mug as he took another sip. "Do you got any aspirin?"

"I think I do somewhere," Ann said. "Did you finish your prescription?"

"I actually stopped taking it the other day. I want to keep a clear head."

"Makes sense. I—uhmm," Ann mumbled while she rummaged inside her purse. "Yeah, here it is."

She handed over the aspirin bottle.

"I just need a couple," Malone said. He poured out four tablets into his palm.

"No, it's fine. Keep it."

"Thanks." Malone put the aspirin by the sink, then came back to the table and watched James finish his donut and lick some of the cream off of his fingers.

"Pretty good, huh?"

"Yeah!" James said. "Mom, can I have one more?"

"That's an awful lot of sugar," Ann said.

"What if we split one?" Malone said to Ann.

She smiled. "Okay. That's fine. As long as I get a bite too."

Malone tore a donut into three pieces and gave a piece to Ann and James. He smiled at James, who had his mouth covered in a mixture of chocolate icing and powdered sugar. Ann had powder on her lip too.

"I don't wanna feel left out," Malone said. He took some of the cream from a donut and wiped it on his own lip, making a mustache.

All three laughed at each other.

"Do you have any napkins?" Ann said.

"Good question." Malone got up from the couch and came back with a near-empty roll of paper towels.

Ann handed a paper towel to James. Then she pulled the last shred of paper towel off and wiped the powder off of her lip.

Malone glanced over at the clock on the microwave. 7:20. "I'm afraid I gotta shower and get ready." Malone finished his donut.

"Come on, James, we better go," Ann said. "We don't want you to be late for school."

James sighed and looked over at Malone.

"See you soon, pal. I'm sorry we couldn't spend more time together this morning." Malone picked up James.

"What if you came over tonight for dinner?" Ann asked.

Malone quickly turned toward Ann. "Absolutely. What time?"

"How's 6:30 sound?"

"That's great," Malone said with a smile. "I'll see you then."

Ann and James started into the hallway.

Malone said, "Wait. Wait." When they turned, he added, "Can I make a request?"

"I guess..." Ann's voice trailed off.

"Let's have whatever this guy wants." Malone pointed at James.

Ann smiled. "I bet we can figure something out. Have a good day."

"You too. See you tonight." He watched them walk down the hallway and then shut the door. Malone took a fast shower and quickly put on a pair of dark jeans, a gray t-shirt, and a black button-down shirt. He slipped on the shoulder holster that held his Sig Sauer P226 and poured the rest of his coffee into a travel mug.

Malone tucked a newspaper under his arm and left his apartment. When he got to his black Chevy Impala, he set the coffee on the roof of the car and slowly stretched his arms over his head. There was almost no pain. The physical therapy must actually be working.

He sipped the coffee as he drove to the 9th District headquarters on South Halstead. Once there, he parked on West 32nd St. and slowly got out of his car. He picked up the paper and glanced over the headlines as he walked. The Bears had the 12th pick in the first round of the NFL Draft. Someone had won the Illinois Powerball for $50 million. Malone shook his head in disbelief. That was a hell of a lot of cash.

Malone's stomach started spinning as he approached the building. He ignored the feeling and walked briskly down the sidewalk as the cold February air hit his face.

Once he saw the entrance, he slowed his stride and stepped into police headquarters. He could feel eyes looking at him and took another sip of coffee. Malone forced a smile as he saw Alex Ramirez, Matt Davis, Jason Wells, and a couple other patrolmen he didn't immediately recognize.

"Welcome back," Ramirez said. He shook Malone's hand firmly. "Ain't the same without you here."

"Yeah, there's one less asshole," Malone smirked.

The others laughed out loud.

"Good to see you," Wells said as he handed a stack of files to Ramirez.

"Malone, welcome back." Davis put his hand on Malone's shoulder.

"Thanks guys. Good to be back."

"Carver wants to see you." Ramirez tucked the files under his arm.

"You know if it's good news or bad news?"

"I'm not sure. Never know with him. Probably both." Ramirez shrugged.

"Yeah, you're right." Malone said quietly. He strolled down the hallway with his coffee in his hand and wished he had some Jameson in it to take off the edge. He ignored the feeling and tapped lightly on Lieutenant Thomas Carver's door. Ever since Malone was in the hospital and they spent that time together, Carver was different. He was more comfortable around Malone and had less of a filter. Maybe he even fully trusted Malone. Carver waved him in, and Malone slowly stepped inside.

"Well, look who's back," Carver stepped around his paper-covered desk and shook Malone's hand. "You look good. Rested. Clearly, some downtime was just what you needed."

"Yeah. It's good to be back."

"As you can imagine, things have changed a little around here while you were out."

"I figured. Are things better or worse?"

"Depends on how you wanna look at it."

"Oh yeah?" Malone asked.

Carver's phone buzzed. He glanced down at it, then looked back at Malone.

"Yeah. Sorry to drop this on you now, but the Gang Task Force was shut down by the brass. You've been moved over to Vice."

"No shit. Guess that's not a surprise, right? It's been on the chopping block for a while."

"Sure has."

"Who's the team leader? Don't tell me it's Cole," Malone said.

"No, it's not Cole. Pretty sure it's, uh, going to be Ramirez. He just passed the sergeant's exam. He doesn't know yet. I thought you could tell him. I think it'd mean a lot coming from you."

"You shitting me?" Malone ran his hand through his hair and looked at the plaque on the wall behind Carver's desk. "Last time I was in here I was asking *you* to bring him over to the Gang Task Force *under* me."

"Yeah, I know. It's a lot of shit to step in just coming back. But it could be a helluva lot worse, right?"

"Yeah, I guess so."

"There's more."

"Always fucking is," Malone mumbled under his breath.

"Vice actually moved into the GTF space."

"Lemme guess. Budget cuts?"

"You know it."

"And you're the supervisor?"

"Afraid not in Vice. I'm working with Narcotics. Your supervisor is Lieutenant Mitchell."

"Vicki? No fucking way. How the hell did she get promoted? Who's she fucking..." Malone's voice trailed off as he collected his thoughts. "Are you kidding me?"

"Afraid not. I know you got some history with her. That gonna be a problem?"

Malone looked out the window and saw Ramirez pass by Carver's office. "No. No. We'll make it work," Malone said with a sigh. "Who do you got in Narcotics?"

"Jason Wells, Matt Davis, David Lopez, Shaun Miller, and Julie Sullivan. Gonna have my hands full for sure."

"Yes, you will."

Carver sighed. "Yeah. And there's been another surge of fentanyl overdoses in town again."

"Really? Not any better?"

"I take it you didn't see the news yet today?"

"Just a couple headlines, but that's it."

"Had fifteen more lethal ODs in a trap house in Washington Park. More of that fentanyl laced shit."

"Fuck. Any leads?"

"Nothing credible. It'll take some time. Brass wants us to work with Cook County Sheriff, which means more meetings and bureaucratic bullshit."

Malone nodded in agreement. "You know, I heard the Gangster Disciples got a fentanyl lab here in town."

"Wouldn't surprise me at all," Carver said as he scratched his signature on a document.

"If you need a hand, just let me know."

Carver looked up at Malone. "Thanks, but you're just coming back. Stay on task. Keep focused. Mitchell's gonna have her eye on you."

"Yeah, you're right." Malone sighed and rubbed his hands on his eyes. "Anything else?"

"I know you been looking hard for Ace like everyone else. I've got Max's former CI keeping an eye out too."

"Good to know. Pretty sure that piece of shit ain't in town. Probably healing up in a dive motel probably in fucking Wisconsin or Kansas." Just saying the words made Malone tighten his jaw and grit his teeth.

"He'll pop up in town sometime."

Malone nodded in agreement. "

"Be careful in Vice. Watch your ass, Malone."

"Yeah. Will do," Malone said. He slowly got up from the chair and left the room.

A few steps later, he stopped by the door at the end of the hall and took a deep breath before entering the office. There was still a Gang Task Force sign on the door which kind of surprised Malone. Once he entered the rectangle-shaped room, he saw Alex Ramirez, David Brown, Ethan Cole, and Victoria Mitchell. Ramirez was a few years younger than Malone. With a youthful face and dark black hair, it was hard to say how old he was other than in his thirties.

Brown was tall and skinny with short brown hair and wore small, rimmed chocolate brown glasses. He was great with computers, but not so great with people. Cole had been on the force for about six years and had quite the reputation as a bit of a party animal. He had short red-brown hair, a boyish face, and a carefree attitude that pissed off more than a few people.

Mitchell was the classic type-A person. Her way or the highway. And she had her sights on the career advancement. Today, her dirty blonde hair was pulled up in a ponytail and she wore a dark pantsuit.

"I suppose congratulations are in order," Malone said and walked toward Mitchell.

"Can it, Malone. Don't give me any of your shit," Mitchell replied.

Malone walked past Mitchell who was sitting at the desk in the middle of the room and approached Ramirez.

"No, I mean this guy. Sergeant? Congrats—really—I mean it," Malone said as he looked at Ramirez.

"What?"

"No one tell you yet? Just heard you passed the sergeant's exam." Malone shook Ramirez's hand.

"Wow. Thanks," Ramirez said.

Mitchell stood up suddenly in the middle of the room. "Mayor Wallace and the deputy chief have high expectations for this unit." She glared at Malone as she spoke. "So, no bull-shit. You'll be following my orders explicitly. If you can't do that, your ass'll be gone. Am I clear?"

All four men nodded their heads in agreement.

"Malone, you're on desk duty until further notice," she said as she walked toward the door.

"Wha—?" Malone stopped himself from saying anything else.

"You heard me. Is *that* a problem for you?" Mitchell turned around.

"No—uh—no. That's not a problem," Malone took a deep breath and sighed, then forced it into a subtle cough.

"Okay, good. I'll leave you to it. Sergeant Ramirez, keep me updated." Mitchell left the room.

"Shit man. I didn't know anything about desk duty or I'd have warned you," Ramirez said.

"That's all right. I just got back," Malone said. "Should take it easy, right?"

"Right. Let the pros go out in the field," Cole said with a scoff as he glared at Malone.

"What the fuck did you say?" Malone sprung out of his chair and got in Cole's face. Malone stared into his eyes. "What'd you say?" Malone asked louder.

"You fucking heard me," Cole said. He grabbed Malone by

the shirt and shoved him. Malone bounced back and pushed Cole, untucking his shirt. Cole crashed into the desk and a stack of paper scattered across on the floor. He charged at Malone and grabbed Malone by the collar of his leather jacket.

"Stop it! Stop that shit now!" Ramirez shouted and slipped in between the two men. Brown lunged forward and grabbed Cole. Cole flailed his arms and Brown got hit on his ear.

Brown was fine, but a bit shaken up and pissed off.

Malone saw this, held his hands up, and quickly backed away.

"I'm just fucking with ya," Cole said in an uneven voice.

"You ain't my type, asshole." Malone said.

"Are we done yet? We got some fucking work to do here!" Ramirez barked.

Cole smiled wide back at Malone. Malone shook his head in disbelief and shifted his eyes back to Ramirez.

"Look," Ramirez said as he walked over to the whiteboard. "Here's where we are. We're doing a prostitution sting, and we're focusing here on the South Side. This is straight from up above, so we gotta deliver on this and get a win."

"World's oldest occupation," Cole said as he looked at the board.

"Where are you looking first?" Malone asked, ignoring Cole.

"The hottest spots."

"So, by Midway and businesses nearby?"

"Yeah. That's one area for sure. Cicero and Archer is also a goddamn hotspot. We've got hookers meeting with johns at Starbucks there," Ramirez said.

"Get blown while sipping your latte, huh?" Malone said.

"Shit, forget the coffee. Definitely worse ways to spend your money," Cole said.

Malone briefly looked at Cole and back at Ramirez. "What's the plan?"

"I'll set up on Archer Avenue, you two'll set up by Midway," Ramirez said to Brown and Cole. Ramirez then picked up a foot-tall stack of files and put them on Malone's desk. "You can go over these."

"What the hell are these?" Malone picked the top file off of the stack.

"Some of the most recent prostitution files we have from the last couple years. Go through 'em, and let me know if you find anything that jumps out at you."

"Yeah," Malone said with a slight sigh as he continued to look at the file.

"You want us to set up anywhere in particular?" Brown asked.

Ramirez looked back to Brown and Cole. Then he said, "Run surveillance at the Marriott. You'll pose as repairmen. There are some coveralls in the back of the van."

Brown and Cole nodded.

"Okay, sounds good," Brown said.

Malone crossed his arms and scowled. "You sure you wanna do that? I know a few hotspots."

"You heard me. You're on the sidelines here. Boss's orders," Ramirez said.

"That's bullshit. Fuck the bosses," Malone replied.

"You want me to tell that to Mitchell? 'Fuck the bosses?'"

"I'm all for having her fuck me," Cole interrupted as he looked over at Lt. Mitchell's office across the hall. "Heard you are too."

"Shut the fuck up," Malone barked at Cole. Then he turned quickly towards Ramirez. "You want results, right? I'm telling you how to get them. All you're gonna do is crack down on some junkies that are shooting up."

"This ain't a discussion." Ramirez said as he turned his back to Malone. "All right. Brown, Cole, let's get going."

Mitchell came back into the room, stopping the men at the door. "Also, the Cook County Sheriff's office will be assisting you with today's operation. You'll need to coordinate with them."

Ramirez nodded as she left. "Okay boys, you heard her. We'll confirm the plan once we talk to the county."

"Sergeant, can I have a word in private?" Malone asked.

"Yeah. Go on ahead," Ramirez said to Cole and Brown.

Malone took a sip of his coffee as he watched the others walk out of the office. Before Cole left, he smirked at Malone, who promptly gave him the finger. Cole scowled back and slammed the door behind him.

Ramirez crossed his arms as he stood in front of Malone.

"Bring me in on this. Don't tie me to the goddamn desk," Malone urged.

"Mitchell's orders. My hands are tied."

"Mitchell don't gotta know," Malone said and took another sip of coffee.

"Look, that ain't how *I* run my unit," Ramirez said. He turned toward the door.

"Then you're gonna fuck this shit up. Just watch," Malone said.

CHAPTER 2

Once alone, Malone looked over at Max's old desk. The same old black computer monitor and the same black chair. File folders and binders still covered the desk. The only real difference was Ramirez's blue and red Cubs mug sitting in the corner. He pictured Max with his feet up on the desk, leaning back with his hands behind head.

Malone then heard the sound of fingers clacking on the keyboard. He turned to his left and saw former GTF team member Leo sitting there. He twisted to his right and saw another former GTF teammate, Johnny, staring right back at him. Malone froze. "What's the plan, boss?" Johnny asked.

Malone felt the air leave his lungs and gasped for another breath, but it wouldn't come. He put his hand on his chest. Time slowed to a crawl. Malone swallowed hard again, finally feeling some air enter his lungs. He slowly counted to ten. When he opened his eyes, the other men were gone.

Leaving the office, Malone went into the restroom and splashed some water on his face. Then he slowly walked back to the office and sat down. He sipped his coffee as he glanced at the paper inside the manila file folder.

The first file was an arrest record from nine months ago. Jerome Williams was arrested for soliciting prostitution at the corner of South Ashland Avenue and 62nd St. Malone looked up the details on the computer. A gas station. Malone leaned forward and looked closely at the photo inside the file. Jerome had a tattoo of the Star of David on his neck, the symbol for the Gangster Disciples. The second file was for Tarsen Green, another Gangster Disciple. He was picked up on Richmond St. Avenue and 65th. Malone knew the area well. That was right by Marquette Elementary School.

The third file was for Erik Marshall. Malone grabbed the fourth folder for Jamele Robinson. He opened another folder and laid it out on his desk on top of the file for Jamele Robinson. Alonzo "Penny" Coleman. Malone knew him. How the hell did Penny get out? Malone put him away a few years ago. He looked closer at the file. Penny was released early for good behavior. "Motherfucker!" Malone growled as he slammed the file shut with this hand. He gritted his teeth and felt his stomach start to spin. Malone got up and walked around the office. He'd been here before. It was part of the job. He didn't have to like it. Not at all. Maybe he could even do something about it. That thought calmed him and he sat back down at the desk.

The next couple hours were a blur as he went through the files for Chris Robinson, Raynell Martin, David Ritchey, Jason Vogel, Stanley Moore, Jacob Miller, and Adonis Jackson. The faces and names started to get jumbled together as he continued making his way through the folders. Malone sighed out loud and stretched his arms over his head.

The phone rang. Malone's eyes darted to the black plastic phone, and he immediately sighed out loud again.

"GT—err—Vice. This is Malone."

"Come to my office. Now," Mitchell said.

"Be right there." Malone slowly rose from his chair and

cleared his throat. He wondered how long it would be before he would have to work with her again. They dated for a few months as rookies. Nothing serious. Out to dinner a couple times. They caught a few movies. They even went out to some bars occasionally. One night, they went to see a local band perform at Metro. After the concert, they each had a couple drinks at the bar. They kissed and kept drinking. They danced into the early morning and spent the night together at her place for the first time. The next morning, Mitchell said she didn't remember anything. She lost it, and Malone quickly left her apartment.

He stopped calling her, which only pissed her off more. Mitchell kept threatening to file sexual assault charges, saying that Malone raped her. Malone couldn't believe it. Everything was consensual. Mitchell never actually filed the charges. She just kept holding it over Malone's head whenever she could. If anything, she became more determined that she had been wronged and she wanted to make things right again by having control over others, now as a supervisor. Malone knew he couldn't trust her, no matter what she said or did.

Through the window, he could see Mitchell sitting at her desk. He knocked lightly on the closed door.

She waved him in. "Sit *down*," she said.

He took a seat in the black chair across from her desk and immediately started to tap his foot.

Mitchell thumbed through a file in her hand. She pulled off her glasses with her free hand and cleared her throat.

Malone crossed his legs and shifted forward in the chair. Whether he leaned forward slightly or slid back a few inches to the backrest, both positions were equally uncomfortable.

Mitchell stood and looked down at Malone. "I know you don't want to be here. Frankly, I don't want you here either," she snapped, slamming the file on the desk.

Malone's eyes widened.

Damn. So much for exchanging pleasantries.

"You know I'm not saying anything new here. So, let's cut the bullshit. I've looked at your file. You've had some wins, but you also make a fucking mess wherever you go."

Malone held his right hand up in protest. "Look—no, I just wanna do some good. I'm taking care of myself, getting my shit together. I ain't gonna be a problem for you. Really."

"You think that bullshit's gonna work on me? We're not back in the academy."

"It ain't bullshit. I'm getting my shit together. I ain't gonna be a problem. If I am, feel free to cut me loose."

"You serious?" Mitchell put her hand on her chin.

"Dead serious," Malone replied, and also stood up.

"No, you're not done here yet. Stay in your seat." Mitchell suddenly moved around her desk and leaned forward in front of Malone. She got close to Malone, just a few inches from his face. Each time he breathed, it was her dead air. He wasn't sure if she was trying to intimidate him or kiss him or what. Malone waited for her to say something, but she stayed quiet. She hovered over him for another moment and then backed away, taking a seat on the corner of her desk.

Mitchell stared back at Malone. In this light, her eyes were dark. She crossed her arms and leaned against the desk. "I heard you're not drinking anymore."

"I'm not," Malone replied.

"Well, maybe not this morning. But you are a liar," she folded her arms in front of her chest.

All of that was a show just to smell my breath.

Malone bit his lip and carefully said, "I ain't lying."

Mitchell stared back at Malone. "You're not turning my unit into a shit show. That means actually following the rules."

"Yeah. Understood."

"Good," Mitchell said with a smile as she sat back down in her chair. "Well, you've got an appointment with the shrink in ten minutes."

"What the—why didn't you tell me earlier?"

"I'm telling you now. You wanna show me you're a team player, prove it to me. Get your ass over there."

Malone nodded in agreement and slowly rose. "Anything else?"

"Don't try any of your bullshit," Mitchell said with a distinct frown. "I'm getting a full report back from the shrink."

"Yeah. Okay," Malone said carefully.

Malone walked out of Mitchell's office with a scowl on his face and hurried down the hall. "Stupid bitch," he mumbled as he opened the men's room door. He knew what she was doing, but it still made him feel like punching the mirror or ripping the hand dryer off of the wall. Malone stared down at the hand dryer and put his hand on the side of it, feeling the cool metal on his fingertips. He took a deep breath and turned toward the sink to splash to some water on his face.

He wished had his flask on him. Then he quickly let the thought float away from his mind. He couldn't do that. Mitchell wanted him to do that. Drinking wasn't an option. What about James and Ann? Drinking would probably get him suspended too. He closed his eyes and tried to focus on something else. The bathroom door flung open, causing Malone to flinch.

"Hey, Malone," Carver said. "How's it going?"

"Just found out I gotta meet with the shrink in like five minutes," Malone grumbled. "Stupid bitch is trying to piss me off."

"Man, you've done this song and dance before," Carver

replied as he walked over to the urinal. "Better to just do it than to stretch it out, right?"

"Yeah, I guess so." Malone dried his hands with the hand dryer for a moment.

Once the hand dryer stopped, Carver continued.

"Don't let her get a rise outta you. That's what she wants." Carver flushed and walked over to the sink.

"Yeah. You're right. Got any aspirin?" Malone rubbed his palm on his forehead and then moved it to the side to massage his temple.

"Yeah. Middle desk drawer. Help yourself. I'll be right there."

"Thanks." Malone followed the hall to Carver's office. He stepped inside and found the aspirin in the middle drawer. He gulped a couple of them down and placed the bottle back in the desk, sitting it next to a book of matches from Dugan's Pub. Malone cleared his throat and quickly shut the drawer.

"You find it?" Carver asked as he entered the doorway.

"Yeah—uh—thanks. Appreciate it." Malone said.

"No problem. You got this. You'll do fine."

Malone half nodded as he glanced at his watch. He had just four minutes until his appointment. "I gotta go," Malone said, as he left Carver's office. He took the elevator to the third floor and found the door to the therapist's office.

When he knocked on the door, a voice inside said, "Come on in."

He stepped into the small but comfortable office. The standard chocolate brown desk was in one corner with a laptop computer on it. The walls had some large, framed photos of tourist spots in Chicago: the United Center, Wrigley Field, and Navy Pier. In front of the desk were two small chairs with black cushions that sat in the middle of the room.

"Hi, I'm Dr. Jill Isley," a woman said from across the room. "You must be Sergeant Ryan Malone. Please have a seat. Make yourself comfortable."

Isley had straight, brown shoulder-length hair and a quiet, almost monotone, voice. She was wearing a gray pantsuit with a pale blue top.

"Nice to meet you," Malone said with a polite smile as he sat down in the small chair.

"Please know that everything you say here is confidential. The only thing I'll be sharing with your supervisor is my recommendation. And I won't go into any real details there."

Malone yawned and then quickly coughed to cover it up. "Okay. Thanks."

"So, how are you doing, Sgt. Malone?"

"I'm good, thanks."

"Good. It's my understanding that you were injured in the line of duty?"

Malone straightened himself in his chair. "Yeah. I—uh—was shot several times about a month and a half ago. I'm fine now. Feeling pretty good."

"Can you expand on that?" Isley asked as she leaned forward in her chair.

"Yeah. I've been on leave for the past six weeks. Have been doing my physical therapy as well and I'm done with that now. I'm honestly just a bit anxious now. I'm ready to get back to work." Malone said. He looked at the framed photo of the Bean over Isley's head and moved his eyes down to look her in the eye.

"Okay. Thanks for sharing. That's understandable. It's always difficult to come back after an injury," Isley said as she scratched something down on her notepad.

Malone sat in silence and realized he was staring at the photo of the Bean again. He would sometimes meet informants there. He shifted his eyes back to Isley and wished he was anywhere else.

"How are your pain levels? It says here were prescribed some medicine for pain, right?"

"I'm doing okay. I was taking oxy-something for pain, but I only took it a couple times."

Isley leaned forward slightly and put her hand under her chin. "Why did you stop using the medication? Were you having cravings to take more of it?"

"No. I just didn't like how it made me feel."

"How did it make you feel?"

"Clouded my thinking. Like I was off in a fog. When that happened the second time, I immediately quit taking it. I want to stay sharp. Haven't had anything but aspirin since then."

"I see. How are you handling stress?"

"Well, I've been working out as much as I can in addition to the physical therapy. Spending more time with the family. Taking my son to a Bulls' game next week. That's about it."

"That's good." Isley said as she wrote something down. "How many hours of sleep are you getting each night?"

"About six hours a night. Something like that," Malone shrugged. "I only get up maybe once or twice during the night."

"I see. Are you currently drinking any alcohol or taking any other form of drug?"

Malone's lip started to quiver. He sensed it and wet his lips.

"No." He shook his head from side to side. "Just coffee and aspirin. That's it." Sweat beaded on Malone's brow, and he looked away from Isley and quickly wiped it off with his hand.

"Good. I only have a few more questions. It's my understanding that you also lost several officers who were very close to you in the line of duty?"

Malone felt the urge to shift in his chair, but remained still. "Yeah, I did. It's hard, but I guess it comes with the job. Ain't nothing I can do about it now." Malone crossed his legs and put his hand in his hair, sensing more sweat on his fingertips.

"Yes. While that's true, it doesn't make it any easier. That's a lot for anyone. How are you handling all of this?"

"I'm fine. Doing okay." His eyes roamed across her desk, where he saw a bottle of apple juice. The color reminded him of Jameson. The way it slipped down his throat, both warm and stinging. Malone wanted a drink. His legs started to feel restless. He wanted to run and hide and be anywhere else but here dealing with this shit.

"I was given your medical records from the hospital. They mentioned that you felt tired and weak with a poor appetite. Have you lost weight over the past month?"

"Ever tried the food over at Mercy Hospital?" Malone said with a chuckle.

"Well, those can be symptoms of problems from alcohol abuse."

"What the hell are you talking about?" Malone blurted out.

"How much alcohol are you consuming now?"

"I told you—I haven't had a drop in over six weeks," Malone snapped.

Isley wrote down something on her notepad.

Malone clinched his teeth and his jaw tightened.

"What about before you were in the hospital? How much were you drinking then?"

Malone bit his lip to unclench his jaw. "I'd just drink on weekends.

Not very much. Just a drink or two. That's it."

"I see," Dr. Isley said as she continued writing. "You mentioned earlier that you've been spending time with your family as a way of relieving stress."

"Yeah, that's right."

"Can you expand on that?"

"Uh—yeah. I'll hang out with my wife and son, watch tv, play games, that kind of thing. Matter of fact, I want to go to a trampoline park soon with them."

"Okay, that's good. Do you feel like you're ready to go back to work?"

"Absolutely," Malone said. He looked at her in the eye and then his eyes drifted to the photo of the Bean again. "I'm definitely ready."

Isley jotted a few words down on her notepad. "Can I ask why?"

"I'm thinking clearly. I'm feeling fine and want to help serve the citizens of Chicago."

Isley wrote several more sentences in her notepad. "Do you have something you'd like to talk about or any questions you'd like to ask?"

Malone sat quietly in his seat, staring back at Isley. He put his palm on his chin, feeling the slight stubble. "No, I'm good." Malone stood up. "When will I know the results?"

"I'll send my assessment to your supervisor as soon as possible."

"Great." Malone shook Dr. Isley's hand and flashed a smile.

Once he was a few doors down the hallway, Malone exhaled deeply. He was relieved it was over, but still pissed at Mitchell. She was trying to push his buttons, and it worked.

Malone left headquarters and climbed into his black Impala. He lit up a cigar, which made him feel a bit better. He glanced at himself in the mirror and noticed his shirt collar was wet with sweat and sticking to his neck. He yawned and wished he was at home in bed. For the past few weeks, he could take a nap whenever he wanted. But not today. He cracked the window hoping the cool February air would help.

As he turned onto Cicero, he remembered the last time he was over in the area. He was just a few blocks away from where the GTF team was ambushed. Johnny and Leo were both shot, and Malone was the only one who made it out alive. He shook off the bad memories, refusing to let his mind play the story again in his mind.

He pulled up to a red light and swallowed hard. Malone knew where he was. He didn't even have to turn his head to know he was by the liquor store in between the nail salon and Jamaican restaurant. The thought popped into his head: just one drink. That'd be just enough to clear his head and get straightened out. Instincts took over. He parked in front of the liquor store and walked in. Once inside, he hurried past the aisles of whiskey, rum, and vodka. He made his way to the cooler and grabbed a six-pack of Budweiser.

Out of the corner of his eye, Malone saw someone else walk into the store. He turned to see a middle-aged man in a navy suit and red power tie. Malone realized it was State's Attorney James Redford. Last time Malone saw Redford, he was with a couple underage prostitutes. Malone squeezed Redford to get Internal Affairs to drop their investigation into him.

Malone watched Redford quickly grab a bottle of Grey Goose vodka, pay with cash, and leave. Malone put the six-pack down on a shelf and hurried back to his car. Redford was driving a government-issued white Chevy sedan that was almost identical to Malone's car, but a few years newer. Malone continued to follow Redford down Cicero. He had a feeling he knew where Redford was going, but at the same time hoped he was wrong. Malone's stomach knotted up as Redford pulled into the Southside Motel parking lot.

Malone hung back and watched Redford go into a motel room with a young woman in a black leather skirt, bright pink top, and shiny silver jacket. He remembered everything that Redford did last time at the same damn place. The screams and the crying. Shit. No. Not again. Never again.

At this moment, Malone wasn't just a cop. He was a father protecting someone else's child. A disgusted taxpayer tired of paying the salary for someone like Redford. He parked across the street and hurried over to the room. With his gun in hand, he kicked in the door.

The girl didn't even scream, which somewhat surprised Malone. She just stood there in front of Redford without saying a word. Redford was in his boxers and undershirt sitting in a faded red chair. The teenage girl was standing topless in front of him with wide eyes.

Redford had a scowl on his face as he turned and faced Malone.

"Do you know who I am?" Redford said.

Malone ignored the question.

"Get dressed. Now." Malone said to the girl.

She slipped on her shirt and then grabbed her purse and jacket.

"Take your money too," Malone said.

She took the cash off of the nightstand and left.

Redford finally spoke. "What—do you know who I am?"

"I do, indeed. Clearly you don't remember me. Here's a quick refresher." Malone punched Redford in the face, hitting him in the cheek.

"Wait! Wait. Why—why the hell are you doing this?"

"It's what you do to the girls, right?"

Malone punched him again, this time in the stomach.

"You beat the shit out of them. You like that, right?"

Malone hit him again, this time with another shot to the other side of his stomach.

Redford gasped for air and coughed as he held his stomach.

"I—I see some girls. So what?"

Malone punched him again in the face, this time hitting Redford hard in the nose.

"So what? You're a sick piece of shit. You abuse underage girls desperate for a fix. That's what."

Malone punched him again, this time with another shot to the other side of Redford's face.

Redford tumbled out of the chair.

Malone felt better until he looked down and saw Redford's bloody face as he was lying on the floor in defeat. It felt all too familiar; like nothing had changed. How many girls had Redford done this to? The thought made Malone want to throw up. This asshole wasn't getting away with this kind of shit anymore. Never again.

Malone drew his P226 from his shoulder holster and pointed it at Redford's head. "I'm tired of your shit, you sick fuck. Give me one reason why I shouldn't kill you right now."

"I got—a family. A wife. A daughter."

"Yeah right, family. Bet your wife wouldn't like to hear about what you do to these girls, huh?"

Malone kept the gun pointed at Redford and picked up the cell phone on the table.

"Wait—wait—wait. Don't. I'll make it worth your while if you just let me go."

"Oh yeah? Is *that* right?" Malone said with a smirk.

"Yeah, I will. How much do you want?"

"How much do you got?"

"I've got a close to a grand. Right here. Let me get it." Redford pulled a wad of cash out of his pants and tossed it on the bed in front of Malone.

"Take it. It's yours. Just leave."

"You can do a helluva lot better than that. I know you're swimming in kickbacks, you dirty fuck."

Malone made a fist and pushed it into his other hand. He watched the vein in Redford's neck throb.

"Look, I don't want no trouble from you—" Redford put his hands up in protest, but looked more like a faith healer.

"Way too late for that."

Malone saw Redford's eyes move to his keys on the table, then he quickly shifted them away.

Malone picked up the car keys and held them in his hand. "Got something in your car, huh?"

"No. No. I just don't wanna be stranded here."

"Yeah, right. Put your clothes on. Now."

Malone scowled as he watched Redford slip into his pants and stuff his feet into a pair of shiny black dress shoes.

"Okay, let's go. Try anything and you'll regret it," Malone said as he put his handgun back into the holster.

"I—I—ain't gonna be no problem," Redford said. He slowly popped his arms into a trench coat and headed toward the door.

Malone walked behind Redford as they stepped out of the motel and walked over towards the white Chevy.

"Tell me something," Malone said.

"What?" Redford asked as he kept walking.

"Why the hell do you do this shit?"

Redford stopped and turned to look at Malone.

"I dunno."

"No, you know. Don't give me that shit. Tell me."

"I—I guess I do it for the same reason anyone does anything. I like it." Redford held a handkerchief to his nose.

Malone felt his thumb press into his index finger and quickly pulled his fist out of his jacket pocket.

Malone grabbed Redford by the coat and pulled him close. "You're a real sick bastard. You know that?"

"I—I never said I was proud of myself."

"You make me fucking sick." Malone pushed Redford away and his back thumped against the side of his car.

"Where the hell is it?" Malone asked.

"Where's what?"

"The money."

Malone got in Redford's face, pushing his back against the car again.

Redford held his hands up as if under arrest. "Again, I don't—want—no trouble..."

"Put your fucking hands down. Where is it? Stop giving me shit," Malone said.

"Okay. Okay. I'll show you."

Malone stepped back out of Redford's way. He was taking too long. People might notice them soon. Malone took a quick glance around, then nudged Redford again.

"It's inside the trunk."

"Open it. Here," Malone tossed Redford the keys.

Redford leaned over, his hands shaking, and unlocked the trunk. Malone tapped his fingers impatiently until he heard the click.

"Get it."

"Wait. You can't—please—don't."

"I don't like repeating myself." Malone glared at Redford.

"Okay—okay. I got it." Redford picked up the bag and handed the bag over to Malone.

"The shit you've done has consequences," Malone said as he looked closer at the trunk. He could shoot him and just leave him right inside the trunk. Better yet, a few blows with the tire iron and it'd be over.

Malone scanned the area, but saw too many cars driving by to like either plan.

"Come on. Back to your room." Malone grabbed Redford and pulled him by the arm across the parking lot.

"You got what you want, just let me go," Redford whined.

"Shut up and move your ass," Malone said as stepped behind Redford and pushed him from behind. Redford stumbled and caught himself before falling over the concrete parking block in the parking lot. Redford started walking again and Malone followed him up to the sidewalk and to the room. He waited for Redford to open the door and then pushed him toward the faded red chair.

"Sit there. Don't fucking move."

Malone set the duffel bag on the bed and unzipped it. The bag was half-filled with cash neatly bound in stacks. It made Malone wonder if Redford had more cash in other locations all over town. He looked over at Redford in the chair. "How much is this?"

Redford's eyes looked away from Malone and stared at the faded green carpet on the floor.

Malone drew his P226 and pointed it at Redford. "I told you I don't like repeating myself, asshole."

"Fifty grand," Redford said with a sigh.

"No shit. Tell you what, I'm gonna take this off your hands."

"Please—don't do this," Redford said. He covered his face with his shaking hands.

"Where's the cash from?"

"I—I can't say. They'll kill me."

"I know it's from kickbacks, asshole." Malone zipped the bag and picked it up. "I got news for you. You're resigning. I don't give a fuck what reason you give. Do it in the next forty-eight hours or your wife and the rest of Chicago is gonna find out what kinda shit you've been doing." He held up Redford's phone. "Remember, I got this too. Willing to bet there's a lot of shit on here." Malone tossed it into the bag's side pocket.

"No! No. Wait. Please don't. You can't do this! This is my job. My career—I need—"

"Wrong. Your former career. If you're lucky, you can go be a telemarketer. No wait, that's too good for you. You can go clean the fucking toilets at Taco Bell."

"Fuck you, you fucking shit," Redford snapped, his voice seething.

The outburst surprised Malone, but didn't stop him from punching Redford in the face. More blood flew from his nose. Malone drew his gun again and pointed it at Redford.

"No. No. Please. I'll do what you say."

Malone kept the gun leveled at Redford's head and weighed the decision.

"Please, no. No."

"Get up," Malone said. Redford slowly got out of the chair, and Malone raised his knee hard, slamming it into Redford's crotch.

Redford groaned and coughed and crumbled again into a ball on the floor.

"I'm not done yet. You're not doing any of this shit again. Either do it my way or I'm gonna have to fix you permanently."

Redford slowly rose up, coughing and shaking.

"No, please. Please."

"Shut up." Malone kneed Redford a second time.

Redford collapsed on the floor again.

"Get up, asshole," Malone said.

"No, no. I can't move. I can't get up. I'm fucking injured here."

"Is that right? I know something that will make that pain go away forever." Malone pressed the gun down on Redford's cheek.

"No. No. I'm getting up."

Redford continued to beg as he slowly stood. The begging disgusted Malone.

He pistol-whipped Redford in the head, knocking him out cold.

"I'm sick of you blabbing so goddamn much," Malone said.

He left Redford in the motel room alone, and hurried to his car, the bag of cash tucked under his arm. He placed it in the trunk of his car and couldn't help but smile as he drove out of the parking lot.

CHAPTER THREE

As Malone drove down the road, he thought about what he'd do with the money. First, some of the cash would go to the families: Max's wife, Jenna, and Leo's wife, Debbie. He also wanted to give some cash to his sister, Sarah. She had a mountain of bills to pay after her son, Andrew, died from a drug overdose. The rest would stay in the storage unit for safekeeping.

Windy City Pawn was ahead, and he decided to stop. Erv was the owner and his information was always reliable. Since the store was located between Latin King and Gangster Disciple turf, he always knew what was going on with both gangs at all times. Erv was in his fifties, and always acted like he was ready to retire at the end of the month. Malone had always wanted to make Erv an official informant, but Erv was too proud to be on a government payroll.

Malone pulled up in front of Windy City Pawn and went inside. The store looked different. Erv had moved some inventory around. Instead of four or five guitars on the wall, there were two, and they were in a different corner. Instead of a row of six or seven bikes, there were three. Even the glass cases didn't have as many necklaces, rings, and watches as usual.

"Bout damn time you came around," Erv said from behind the glass counter. He was wearing a long-sleeved dark red button-down shirt and black pants. He had an ever-present toothpick in his lips. Erv was holding a newspaper and folded it in half before he set it down on the counter.

"First day back in the saddle," Malone replied.

"So, your ass hurts, right?" Erv laughed.

Malone nodded with a chuckle. "How you doin, Erv?" Malone said.

"Better 'an you, but that ain't sayin much, is it?"

Malone smiled.

"Man, I think you got something on your shirt," Erv said.

"What's that, man?"

"On your t-shirt. Looks like maybe barbeque sauce. You eatin a shit ton of ribs or something?"

Malone pinched his gray t-shirt with his thumb and index finger and noticed a few drops of blood near the collar. Malone exhaled and then shook his head in disgust. "Damn, think you caught me." Malone said with a small chuckle. He pointed at the wall. "You don't—uh—got a lot of inventory here."

"You not hear?"

"Not hear what? I've been out of the loop for a few weeks."

"Those goddamn gangs been at it again. They been recruiting and everyone's gotta prove how tough they are. Got held up a couple times over the past few weeks, so I ain't buying nothing."

Malone bit his lip. "Really? That's bullshit. We talking Latin Kings and Gangster Disciples?"

"Yep. Even a few Vice Lords been stirring up shit too."

"I didn't hear anything about any of this. Civilians hurt?"

"I'm sure a few have. But that ain't something gonna be on the unless they white or got a lotta money, huh."

"Yeah, I hear you." Malone nodded. "Quiet now?"

"Yep. Has been for the past couple days. Maybe too quiet. Now I just need some more customers to come in, buy some shit, ya know?"

Malone smiled.

"Speaking of which, how 'bout this bracelet for your girl?"

Malone eyed the shiny silver bracelet in the black box.

"That's a tennis bracelet. Sterling silver. Total diamond weight of 1/3 carat. You know she'd like this, man."

Malone knew he was right. "How much you want?"

"I can do $250 for ya."

"Let me think about it. You know a Gangster Disciple named Ace?"

"Yeah, I know Ace."

"Any idea where he is?"

Erv scratched his chin. "I dunno. I ain't seen him in a long time."

"Yeah, all I know is he's been in the wind. Anything at all could really help me out."

"If he's hidin, you just gotta wait that nigga out. He'll come out when he's hungry, right?" Erv said.

Malone nodded. "Yeah. Let me see that bracelet."

Erv pulled the bracelet out of the jewelry case and handed it to Malone.

"Ann would like this, you're right. I'll do $200."

"Come on, man. Help a brother out," Erv said with wide a smile.

"I only got $200 on me, man. I'm a civil servant on a government salary. That's all I got. Really."

"Fine, fine. Deal." Erv put the jewelry in a bag for Malone.

Malone handed over a wad of cash to Erv, who unfolded it and started counting the money. Malone headed to the door.

"Thanks. Lemme know if you hear anything I should know, will you?"

"Yeah, will do."

"Appreciate it."

"Wait, man," Erv said as he counted the cash. "This is almost a grand here."

Malone nodded his head once and flashed a smile.

"Maybe you all right after all. You know that?" Erv smiled back.

As he climbed back in his car, Malone thought more about what Erv said. Malone may have weakened both gangs by taking out their leaders, but the violence—and the death that it brought—wasn't going anywhere.

Malone drove down Cicero and noticed the prostitute from Redford's motel room standing on the side of the road. He offered her a ride, but she declined. He thought about giving her some more money, but knew every penny would be spent on getting high.

As Malone drove down the road, he decided to check in with Ramirez. Malone cleared his throat. "Hey, it's me. Where are you now?"

"Next to a muffler shop on Archer," Ramirez said.

"Well, I'm at lunch. Can I bring you or the other guys some coffee or a sandwich or something?"

"Man, Mitchell benched you. That shit ain't gonna work on me."

"What the fuck are you talking about? I was just trying to—"

"That ain't how I do things, Malone. I know what you're doing. Get your ass back to the office."

Malone hung up and slammed his hands on the steering wheel, letting out a growl. Stupid asshole. Malone looked at the time. 1:05. He'd been gone an hour, but he was also the only one in the office, so what did it matter?

Instead of going back to headquarters, Malone drove down the Magnificent Mile and turned onto W. Kinzie. He pulled into a small parking lot by the brick building filled with storage units. He scanned the parking lot. It looked like the storage building was mostly empty. Malone slipped on a White Sox hat and pulled it down low, hiding most of his face. He quickly hurried to the trunk and grabbed the duffel bag.

The last time he'd been here felt like forever ago. He had set aside some cash from a Latin Kings drug bust and hadn't really thought about it much since. But now that he was there outside of the storage unit, he found himself hoping that the cash was safe. Malone typed a four-digit pin code on the door that unlocked the glass door. He climbed onto the elevator and tried to remember how much cash was already inside of the storage unit. He thought it was around thirty or forty grand, but he couldn't remember.

As the elevator rose, he noticed he was having some heart palpitations. He tapped his foot on the floor to distract himself. On the third floor, he exited and turned right. Stopping in front of his unit, he pulled his keys from his pocket and searched for the one to unlock the storage unit. His keys dropped and fell with a loud bang.

"Shit!" He grabbed them, found the right one, and slid it into the padlock. He turned the key, but the lock wouldn't open. He tried again and the key wouldn't budge.

"Motherfucker!"

He continued to wiggle the key back and forth. Malone could feel his jaw tightening as he continued to work on the lock. Without warning, the key snapped in the lock.

"Son of a bitch!" He looked down at the tiny stub that remained of the broken key. He cursed again in disgust.

His phone rang and he glanced down at it to see an unfamiliar Chicago number. He pressed ignore to send it to voicemail and grabbed the bag of cash, slinging it over his left shoulder. He took the elevator down to the first floor and made his way to the office at the end of the building. A sign on the door read out to lunch.

Malone felt like punching the wall or screaming at the top of his lungs. But he saw his reflection in the office door and remembered there were many cameras in the building. He had to be smart. He stormed out to his car and popped the trunk. Inside he found a blanket, a first aid kit, a portable defibrillator, body armor, a shotgun, and some ammo. That was it. He thought he had a pair of bolt cutters, but they weren't there.

Malone grunted out loud as he slammed the lid to the trunk. He hurried back to the storage unit again, the bag slung over his right arm. Once there, he pulled hard on the door. The door moved slightly, but the broken lock kept the door stuck on the floor. The idea crossed his mind to pull out his gun and to shoot the lock off of the door, but he knew that was a dumb idea. Malone felt sick as his eyes focused on the broken lock. There was too much cash on the line to make a stupid mistake here.

Just then, he remembered there was a hardware store close to Merchandise Mart. He could run over there and come right back with a pair of bolt cutters and a new lock. Just knowing that was an option took a weight off of Malone's shoulders. He left the storage unit and set the duffel bag in the passenger seat as he drove to the hardware store.

His phone rang again, but he left it in his pocket. First things first. The hardware store was located in a strip mall next to a drugstore and a pet store. Three parking spaces were in the front—all filled—and a paid lot was off to the side behind the stores. The sidewalk, however, was very flat in front of the stores, so Malone made his own parking space to the right of the vehicles.

He ran into the hardware store and quickly grabbed a pair of bolt cutters off of the shelf and a new silver padlock. After paying at the register, he looked outside and saw a uniformed police officer standing outside by his car. *Shit,* he thought. *The bag of cash is right there on the passenger seat.*

"Hey there," Malone said, rushing out. He held up his badge. "Just had to swing by for some shit for my supervisor. Asshole likes to think I'm his errand boy sometimes."

The officer looked up at Malone and tucked his clipboard under his arm.

"I hear you. My boss is like that too. Really sucks."

"Yeah, you said it. Have a good day."

Malone got into his car and fought the urge to think about what just happened. Thinking about it more would just make him want a drink. Instead, he sped back to the storage unit and focused on dropping off the cash. Nothing else mattered. When he pulled up to the storage unit, no new cars were parked outside and that comforted him as he went back inside.

He took the elevator up to the third floor and his reflection on the wall revealed how much he was sweating. His shirt collar was dark and matted down. His hair was flattened and his face was wet. Malone wiped his forehead with the back of his arm and refocused his attention on the job at hand.

His phone vibrated in his pocket again, but he continued to ignore it. He grunted as he squeezed the bolt cutters tight against the padlock. It took a few tries, but he was able to get it off. Malone then slipped the new lock on the door and carried the cash inside. He walked toward the blue and green plastic bins piled up in the back of the storage unit. He opened them and saw the stacks of cash inside and flipped through it. All the cash appeared to be there. And now he was adding even more to it.

Malone poured out the cash from the duffel bag into the last green bin, and smiled at the stacks of cash only a few inches from the top. Not a bad problem to have.

As he walked out of the storage unit, Malone glanced down at his phone to see who had called. One call was from area code 414. He had two other calls from the same unknown Chicago number. No voicemails from any of the calls. Malone decided to try calling the Chicago number as he drove back to headquarters.

"Hello? Someone just called me from this number?"

"Malone, where the hell are you?"

He recognized the voice. Mitchell.

"Hey. I was, uh, just grabbing lunch."

"When I call, you answer. Do you hear me?"

"Yeah. Didn't know it was you. You didn't leave a message."

"Well, now you know it's me. Come to my office. Now."

"Yeah. I'm on my way back. I'll see you in a minute," Malone said, ending the call. With a deep groan, he slapped his hands on the top of the steering wheel.

Malone pulled up in front of the headquarters and looked at himself in the mirror. He was still sweaty from the storage unit and tried to soak up some of the sweat using some fast food napkins from the glovebox. They didn't help much, but it was better than nothing. He noticed the blood spots again on his shirt. Fuck! He meant to grab another t-shirt from the storage unit. Too late now. He buttoned his top collar button, but it looked too formal. He then unbuttoned his shirt and grabbed the t-shirt collar and stretched the fabric, pulling the shirt down so the blood stain was hidden. That would have to do. He took a couple deep breaths and hurried back to the office. When he walked in the door, he found Mitchell in the Vice office sitting in his chair.

"Where the hell were you?" Mitchell asked. She stood up and moved her hands to her hips.

"Lunch. Got a dog at Portillo's. Want the receipt?"

"I see. Come here." Mitchell motioned with her index finger.

Malone stepped closer. She held out a black rectangle-shaped breathalyzer.

"You said you're gonna be a team player. Prove it to me," Mitchell insisted.

Malone took the breathalyzer and blew into it. He handed it back to Mitchell.

She looked at the numbers on the breathalyzer and then back at Malone. "Good. Now keep it that way or your ass is gone."

"Yes, Lieutenant," Malone droned.

"Get back to work." Mitchell walked out of the Vice office and glanced back with a quick smirk.

Malone stared back in disbelief and sighed out loud as the door closed. She was getting worse and seemed to be enjoying every minute of it. Still, he had a job to do.

Malone went through more files for the next couple hours and marked the locations on a map of Chicago with thumb-tacks. Yellow for Latin Kings, blue for Gangster Disciples and red for other gangs. No clear patterns were on the map. Malone sighed and rubbed his eyes. Then he got some coffee from the break room and stopped by Carver's office door.

Carver was on the phone, but waved him in. "Yeah, yeah. Look, I gotta go. Bye."

"Sorry to bother you," Malone said, "but can I get some more aspirin?"

"Here," Carver said. He pulled the bottle out and tossed it to Malone. "It's fine. Keep it."

"Thanks," Malone said with a smile.

"Take a seat. Wild first day back, eh?" Carver leaned back in his chair and put his hands behind his head.

Malone rubbed his palms on his face. "Yeah, you could say that."

"Hang in there, you know? First day back's a real pain in the ass, ain't it?"

"Sure is." Malone nodded.

"How'd it go with the shrink?"

"Not too bad. Supposed to get the results soon. Probably tomorrow."

"That's a quick turnaround there. She must like you or hate you. Ain't many civil servants moving that fast."

Malone shrugged his shoulders. "Well, sitting around waiting for something to happen is bullshit."

"Tell me about it," Carver said with a smile. "You ain't done yet. Try and be patient. Give it some time."

"I'm trying, man. Not one of my strengths." Malone smiled at Carver as he left his office.

Malone realized that the Vice office felt bigger when he was the only one there. He sat back down at his desk and went through some of the files again. There wasn't much of anything in common with these cases other than prostitution. He stared at the clock on the wall and wondered if he came back to work too early. The urge to lay his head down on the desk was very real as his eyes glazed over. The only thing that made him feel a little better was knowing that Redford was about to retire. Malone's cell phone rang, and the name Ann flashed on the screen.

"Hey," Malone said. "Are we still on for dinner?"

Ann didn't respond.

Malone heard the sound of sniffling. "You okay?"

"You know Marie Bauer?" Ann said with her voice trembling. "Noah's mom?"

"Yeah, I think I know her," Malone replied, as he tried to disguise a yawn.

"Marie was helping with a class party today. She got shot leaving the school. There were a few windows shot out too."

"Shit, I'm so sorry." Malone put a fist to his mouth and swallowed hard. Almost immediately, anger swelled up in his gut.

"Yeah—I dunno where they took her."

Malone felt his jaw tighten and he bit his lip. "Where are you at now?"

"I'm in the car, on my way to pick up James from school."

Malone got up and stuffed a few file folders under his arm.

"I'll meet you. See you in a minute." He hurried out of the Vice office. Out of the corner of his eye, he saw Mitchell in her office. He didn't say anything and rushed out of police headquarters.

Driving down South Halstead Street, he flipped on the siren as he sped by some other cars and cut down Ashland Avenue to West 13th Street. As he pulled over to park on the street, he called Ann. "Where are you now?"

"I'm getting James from his classroom. I'll meet you right outside the main entrance, okay?"

"Okay," Ann said and then hung up.

Malone saw two uniforms sitting in a squad car and walked toward them. The driver was Al Baldwin, and the passenger was John Cruz.

"Hey, Malone," Cruz said.

"What the fuck happened? My kid goes to school here," Malone said.

"Looks like a drive-by. Witness said it was a red Toyota Camry. One pedestrian was shot in the leg and taken over to University Hospital. We're just here tying things up here," Lopez said.

"Anyone else hurt?"

"Nope."

"Any leads?"

"Found some 9mm casings for the lab. Two witnesses said they saw two young males, both Latino. That's what we got so far."

"I see." Probably new gang members looking for street cred, Malone thought. He leaned forward. "Statements say anything about tattoos or gang colors?"

Wells looked down at the two witness statements and scanned them. "Nothing mentioned here."

Malone rubbed his hand on his chin and spat on the ground.

"We also got an APB out on that red Camry," Baldwin said.

"Okay. Lemme know if you get anything else."

"Will do," Cruz said.

Malone stepped away from the cruiser. Only a few hundred red Camrys in Chicago, he thought. A needle in a haystack.

Ann and James walked out of the school. Ann was holding his hand and had bloodshot eyes.

Malone met them on the sidewalk and forced a smile. "Hey, pal." He picked up James in his arms.

James said hi, but other than that stayed really quiet. The sound of gunfire that close obviously scared him. Ann didn't say much either as she walked to her blue minivan.

"Let's get you home, buddy," Malone said to James.

As Ann buckled her seatbelt, she asked, "Did you find out anything about Marie?"

"She's at University Hospital and got hit in the leg. That's all I know."

Ann shook her head in disgust. "I wanna go see her."

"Want me to drive you over there?"

"No, I'm fine. But can you take James back to the house? And maybe figure out something for dinner?" Ann asked.

"Sure. I'll get his seat." Malone carefully set James down next to him, and then pulled the booster seat from the back-seat of the minivan.

"We'll see you back at the house," Malone said, as he held the booster seat in his arms.

"Bye, hun," Ann said to James.

James didn't reply and took his booster seat to the car.

Ann motioned to Malone to come closer, and dropped her voice. "Things are only getting worse. Everyone's getting shot or..."

"Yeah. I know," Malone's lip quivered as he spoke.

Ann left, and Malone stood in the street next to his car as he watched Ann walk away.

CHAPTER 4

Redford opened his eyes feeling sore as hell and lightheaded. He could barely move. His head hurt. His face hurt. His nose hurt. His jaw hurt. His back hurt. His groin hurt. Everything hurt.

He drank more vodka to distract himself from the pain. The room started to spin and he passed out again. This time when he woke up, he checked the time. Almost three hours had passed. He was a bit dizzy and his confusion turned into rage. Not only did this cop take his cash, but he was also trying to take away his identity, his career, his security, and his future. Everything he had been working for over the years. This goddamn cop wasn't going to just go away. He had popped up twice in the last few months and made life miserable both times. He damn near killed him this time.

Once the dizziness started to fade, he cleaned himself up as best he could, threw away his bloody white t-shirt, and carefully put on his white button-down Oxford shirt. Redford slipped on his trench coat and walked out to his car. He remembered he had some painkillers in the center console and immediately gulped down a handful of them. As he drove down the road, he thought about all of the possible scenarios of what could happen.

Sure, he could resign. But even retiring meant he likely couldn't stay in Chicago. This cop was a major pain in the ass. He'd have to move somewhere else. Fuck that. He knew what to do. He pulled over in front of a cellphone store, hurried inside, and bought a burner phone. Redford pulled the phone out of the plastic package and dialed a number that he had memorized.

"Yeah. It's Redford. I need to talk to you."

"Why the hell you callin' me?" the voice said.

"I need help. I—got a problem." Redford took a sip of vodka.

"No shit you got a problem. You a crazy asshole."

Redford ignored the insult. "Look, Diego, it's important."

"Not on here. In person, you dumb fuck."

"This phone's clean. Where—where—are you?"

"No man. I'll come to you."

"Okay. Usual place?" Redford asked.

"Yeah, I know where ya mean. Gimme half an hour."

Redford hung up and felt the acid whirl around in his stomach. He took another drink of vodka and wished he could still be back at the motel with the girl.

Redford dialed Laurie's number, but she didn't pickup. When it went to voicemail, he hung up. He thought about going home to get a change of clothes, but remembered an extra shirt in the car. That taken care of, he drove to the metallic bean-shaped structure over in Millennium Park.

His throat was dry and he swallowed hard, hoping it would make the stuffy cotton feeling go away. He pulled into the garage and found a parking spot between a white Honda SUV and a gray Ford sedan. He held the vodka bottle up to his lips and finished it off. Carefully, he tucked the bottle under the driver's seat and slowly got out.

As usual, there was a large crowd standing around "The Bean" in Millennium Park. People were posing in front of the large metallic bean-shaped structure and taking photos. A field trip of middle schoolers stood by it and the teacher was reading some facts out loud. Downtown workers breezed through the park, taking a walk or heading out to grab lunch.

Redford saw Diego off in the distance sitting alone on a bench. Redford could barely walk. It was more of a limp. A group of young Mennonite women in powder blue dresses walked by. He could feel their eyes on him. Redford spilled onto the bench at the other end opposite Diego.

Diego was of average height, but well-built and clearly worked out. He was wearing a crisp white t-shirt, a thick gold chain, and black Adidas track suit.

Diego didn't look directly at Redford. "What the hell ya want?" he asked as he took a drag from his cigarette and exhaled the smoke. He pushed his free hand through his short dark hair, making it stand up.

"This uh, fucking cop—Ryan Malone—wants me to resign. If I don't do it, he's gonna send incriminating photos to the newspapers and my family," Redford said.

"None of this shit matters to me. Why you wasting my time?" Diego was watching a group of teenage girls posing by the Bean for a photo.

"I—I'm not. I lose my job, I can't help you anymore."

Diego stomped out his cigarette on the ground. "Look, I'm here 'cause of the old man. I ain't got no say with any of this shit you talkin about."

"Just tell 'em about my problem."

Diego turned toward Redford without saying a word.

Redford fought the urge to look away, but kept his eyes on Diego.

"What's this cop's name again?"

"Malone. Sergeant Ryan Malone."

Diego wrote down the name on his hand, and said, "I find out you lyin', you ain't gonna like it."

The color drained from Redford's face. "I'm not lying," Redford said.

"Keep it that way, or you gonna regret it." Diego opened his jacket to reveal his 9mm tucked in the waist of his pants.

"I—I will," Redford stammered. Redford swallowed hard to fight back the urge to vomit, which made it sound like he was choking. He bent over and spat on the ground.

"Good," Diego said. He sprung up from the bench and walked away.

Diego knew not to trust Redford at all. Any kind of politician can't be trusted. Let alone one who liked to go to get drunk in sleazy motels with underage prostitutes.

Diego had no problem with women himself. The idea of paying for sex was something he could never understand. As he walked down North Michigan Avenue, he pulled out his phone.

"We got a problem," Diego said.

"I see. What's the problem?" José replied. José was in his late fifties and dressed immaculately in a dark gray suit with a powder blue shirt and a blue and orange tie. Behind his desk was the incredible view that came with having an office on the seventieth floor of the Willis Tower. He stood up and looked out the window, glancing down at the Chicago Board of Trade building. It looked so small from where he stood.

"Redford says a cop is blackmailing him. Says he gotta retire or this cop will go to the media."

"That is a problem. What's the officer's name?"

"Malone. Sergeant Ryan Malone."

"All right. I'll look into this matter," José said as he smoothed his tie.

Diego hung up and continued to walk down Michigan Avenue.

CHAPTER FIVE

Malone wasn't surprised that James wanted him to turn on the siren as soon as he started the car. "I can't, buddy. It's only for official police business."

"Come on, Dad. Turn it on. You know you wanna."

Malone laughed. "We're not that far from the house. It'll only take a minute."

"I'm hungry."

"Shi—shoot. Yeah, I'll get you something to eat," Malone said as he lightly slapped the steering wheel with his right hand.

"Dad, I know that means cereal or pizza."

Malone laughed. "That's possible. Tell you what, I'll turn on the siren just for a little bit."

A moment later, as Malone parked in front of the two-story brick house, he yawned and realized how tired he was. He unlocked the door and stepped into the house. James and Malone watched some cartoons and ate cereal. As Malone got up to take the dishes to the kitchen, Ann walked in. Both Malone and James greeted her, but she just waved quickly without saying a word. She walked through the living room and went directly upstairs.

"I think Mom needs to rest, pal," Malone said to James. They continued to watch TV together for the next half hour.

Malone got up from the couch and visited Ann in the bedroom. She was lying flat in bed on her stomach but moving. "Can I get you anything?"

She didn't answer.

"Look, I know you're upset. But how is not talking going to help anything?"

Ann turned toward Malone and glared at him. "That's fucking hilarious coming from you. For the past few years, it's been like talking to a wall. And that's when you're actually around."

"You—you're right. I know. I've fucked up." Malone sat on the bed and exhaled deeply. "I've taken you for granted and only cared about the job. I know. I'm sorry."

Ann's eyes widened as Malone put his hand on her back. She took a deep breath and just watched him.

"How's Marie doing?"

"Seemed all right. They gave her some Vicodin, so she wasn't feeling a thing. She was just sleepy and drowsy."

"Makes sense. Glad she's okay." Malone slowly stood up and took a deep breath. "So, we had cereal for dinner. I'm sure that's just what you want."

Ann laughed. "Whatever. That's fine."

James was still watching television when Malone and Ann came down the stairs. Ann sat down on the couch and put her arm around James. Malone went into the kitchen and soon came back with a bowl of Cheerios for Ann.

"I was betting on this, pizza, or peanut butter and jelly sandwiches."

"Dad forgot to get dinner," James blurted while he watched tv.

"Thanks for backing me up, pal," Malone said with a chuckle.

Ann laughed.

The three hung out on the couch watching *101 Dalmatians*. About halfway into the movie, Malone fell asleep and started snoring loudly.

"Dad sounds like a grizzly bear," James said.

"You're right. But let him rest for a minute," Ann said with a smile. Ann and James continued to watch the movie.

Malone woke up to the sound of his phone ringing. It was Ramirez.

"Yeah?" Malone said, as he wiped his eyes with his index finger.

"Something came up with the team from the county sheriff. Could use some help here."

"Where are you?" Malone asked.

"Archer and Cicero. Muffler shop across from Starbucks."

"I'm on my way."

Malone turned to Ann and James. "I'm sorry, but I gotta go. They need my help." He kissed James on the head and hurried to the door.

"Wait," Ann said as she followed Malone to the door.

"Look, please don't give me any shit about this," Malone said under his breath.

"Don't forget to get his booster seat out of your car," Ann answered him coldly.

"Oh yeah." Malone hurried out and got the booster seat from the car and brought it back to Ann. She took it and shut the door.

After speeding down Cicero, Malone turned into the muffler shop's lot and pulled up next to the black GMC van. Malone saw Ramirez behind the steering wheel. He nodded toward Ramirez, who lowered the window.

"Get yourself a new ride, eh?"

"Yeah. Well, new to me I guess," Ramirez said. "Kinda smells like ass in here, though."

Malone laughed. "Come on, that's just the smell of fast food and good ol' fashioned police work," Malone said. "See any action?"

"Surprisingly quiet. Too cold out for anyone to be outside."

"So, you're just lonely and need some company, huh?"

"Yeah, yeah." Ramirez said. "Actually, we're gonna meet up with Brown and Cole at the Marriott. Follow me."

Ramirez left and Malone followed close behind. After driving down Cicero for a couple of blocks, Ramirez pulled into the Marriott parking lot and found an empty parking spot in the corner.

Malone parked a few spaces down then walked over to Ramirez's van and got inside.

"We're outside. Do you copy?" Ramirez said into his radio.

"Yeah, loud and clear," Cole said.

"Any contact from our CI?" Ramirez asked.

"No, but three girls have stopped by Room 207 over the past half hour," Cole replied, "and two stayed there."

"Okay. Hold your position."

Malone looked over at Ramirez. "Cash drop?"

"Looks like it," Ramirez replied.

Both men were quiet until Malone asked, "This is a weird gig, don't you think?"

"What's weird?" Ramirez asked.

"Prostitution. We're all getting fucked by someone for money," Malone smirked.

"Man, that's pretty cynical. But I suppose that's one way to look at it."

Malone looked over at the hotel. "I wonder if we can see into the room from the outside."

Ramirez turned and looked at the windows. Most of the rooms had the blinds open. "Yeah, maybe we can. Let's go check it out."

Malone nodded and got out of the car. He followed Ramirez through a side door and down the hallway on the first floor of the hotel. It led to the lobby, which had a few chairs, a sectional sofa, and some square stools surrounding a large fireplace. Two large columns were in the middle of the lobby. As Malone walked in, he stopped by the large fireplace. Out of the corner of his eye he saw three Latino men step in through the main entrance.

He quietly called out to Ramirez. Then the two men slipped behind the large wooden column by the fireplace.

Once the men left the lobby and started down the hallway, Ramirez pulled out his radio. He said, "Take cover. You may have some company heading your way from the lobby. Looks like three Latin Kings."

"Copy that," Brown said.

Cole and Brown took cover standing beside the ice machine.

"Don't see anything yet," Brown said into the radio.

"Stay ready," Ramirez replied.

Several minutes passed. All of the men waited silently.

"Maybe they're here for action from the girls too," Ramirez said.

"Yeah, maybe," Malone replied.

Malone and Ramirez slowly stepped out from behind the column and dashed to the other hallway and climbed up the stairs. They found Cole and Brown in the area by the ice machine.

"See those three guys yet?" Malone said.

"Nope," Brown said as he looked at the camera in his hands.

"How many inside the room?" Ramirez asked.

"Not sure. At least two girls inside," Cole said as he rubbed his palm on his chin.

"We really need some eyes on the inside," Ramirez said.

"I can't get the camera to work," Brown replied.

"Might be able to see something from the outside," Malone said.

"That's the second time you've mentioned something about that. You volunteering?" Ramirez said.

Malone laughed. "First day back and you want my ass dangling off a balcony in the snow and ice? Fuck that."

Ramirez smiled and then tilted his head. "It ain't that high up, you know? Besides, it was your idea. Here's the master key." He held it out on his palm.

"Fuck you very much," Malone said as he took the key.

"Asshole." Ramirez said with a smile as he watched Malone step into Room 201.

Malone hurried through the hotel room, then slowly walked out onto the balcony. Once he got outside, the cold air hit him in the face. He climbed carefully onto the other side of the railing. "Stupid lazy bastards," he mumbled.

The wind blew through his leather jacket and cut deep. He looked over at the ledge and saw a portion of the roof hung out in front of the first floor. It was about six feet to the right. Malone stared at the ledge, then jumped over the clearing and landed awkwardly on the other side.

Slowly, Malone moved past the first room. He then approached the second, which had the blinds closed. In the third room, he could see the light was on in the window. The blinds were partially open. Not much, but maybe enough for him to see something. He made his way forward, watching his footing as he walked across the roof. In the window, he saw a large man dressed in a black jacket with his back near the window. He continued to look inside, but couldn't see anything else.

Bang. A loud noise popped behind him. It was really close. Malone didn't have time to move or react. He just fell down to his knees as his stomach sank, like he had been punched hard in the gut.

CHAPTER SIX

The same loud noise again. It was a car backfiring in the parking lot. Malone exhaled and shook his head in disbelief. He definitely came back to work too soon. Malone moved to the ledge and dug his heels into the ground. He placed one hand on his chest and took a measured breath. His eyes moved to the balcony, and he leaped into the air. He made it across, but hit his right arm—the one with the fresh skin graft—on the black metal railing. Malone climbed over the railing and held his arm as it throbbed in pain. He wanted to scream, but muffled the sound into his fist. Malone walked into the hotel room and sat on the bed. He pulled the small aspirin bottle out of his inner jacket pocket, and gulped down four small white tablets. After a minute, Malone slowly rose to his feet and walked through the room back to the hallway.

Ramirez, Cole, and Brown were waiting by the vending machine.

"I just saw the back of one guy. Looked like he was waiting for something. Had some white powder on the desk too near the window."

Ramirez nodded. "Okay, that's enough for probable cause."

"See anything out here?" Malone said as he handed the room key to Ramirez.

"Nothing yet," Ramirez replied and pocketed the key.

"Guys from the lobby?" Malone asked.

"Nope. Nothing." Cole shrugged.

Brown tapped the side of the tactical camera with his hand. "Come on, come on."

"Problem?" Malone asked.

Brown sighed. "The image keeps cutting out."

"Great." Malone flicked his eyes over to Ramirez and sighed quietly.

"You think something is going down?" Ramirez said.

"They're definitely waiting on something," Malone replied.

Sweat beaded on his forehead and he wiped it off with the back of his left hand.

"You okay?" Ramirez said.

"Yeah. I, uh—" Malone held his index finger up to his lips and then pointed.

The sound of footsteps echoed in the hallway.

Ramirez held up a small mirror and saw a young woman approaching. She had curly brown hair and was wearing a black miniskirt with a red low-cut top.

"Saw her earlier. She's one of the girls," Cole whispered.

"Something's in her hand," Ramirez said quietly.

The girl went inside Room 207.

All four men waited. The ice machine started up and whirred loudly next to them. It blew out hot air and soon sweat beaded on their foreheads.

Ramirez watched the door, ready to duck for cover at a moment's notice.

The girl in red came out of the room and walked down the hallway toward the elevator.

"She just took the elevator down," Ramirez said.

"If that camera won't work, can we get another one?" Malone asked.

"This is it. Here. You're welcome to try." Brown said. Then he handed the tactical camera to Malone.

Malone turned off the camera and bit his lip as he waited for it to boot up. If this didn't work, his next plan was to kick down the door.

Malone saw an image of the ice machine on the camera's small LCD screen. "Think I've got it." Malone turned toward Ramirez. "Maybe we should have someone by the elevators?"

"Good idea. Cole, keep an eye out," Ramirez said.

Cole nodded in agreement and hurried down the hallway to where he had a better view of the elevator.

Malone and Ramirez moved over to the hotel room door behind Brown. Brown positioned the tactical camera on the ground to slip it under the door. Ramirez had the battering ram in his hands and Malone had his P226 drawn.

The camera screen turned black. Brown smacked the camera with the palm of the hand, and it stayed black. "Work, you stupid piece of shit," Brown mumbled.

Cole walked down the hallway toward the two elevators. Across from them was a table with a lamp and a telephone, and tall plants on each side. He really didn't have anywhere to hide that was out of view, so Cole just stood to the side of the hallway where he could easily turn to the door and act like he was about to enter. As he stood there, his stomach started to grumble and he wished he had eaten something besides junk food in the car. The elevator chimed. He waited, but no one got off. "Shit," he mumbled. He rubbed his eyes and continued to keep watch.

Brown smacked the camera again and the screen lit up

showing a blonde prostitute sitting on the bed and two men sitting in chairs. Brown nodded to Ramirez and quickly pulled the camera back from the door.

Ramirez swung the battering ram hard, breaking open the hotel room door.

Inside the room was another prostitute, a brunette wearing red lingerie. She screamed and dropped some empty beer bottles onto the ground, startling everyone. On the other side of the room, a Latino man sat at a table counting stacks of cash. He turned around to see what had happened. Malone immediately recognized him. It was Ramon Garcia Jr., also known as King Jay or Junior. With his thin black beard, slicked back hair, and dark eyes, he looked a lot like a twenty-two-year-old version of his grandfather, Ramon, the leader of the Latin Kings.

"Shit," Junior said and dropped the stack of cash onto the floor. He reached over a mirror with a few lines of coke on it and picked up a shiny, chrome-plated Glock. He held the gun sideways and quickly fired several shots at Malone, but missed wide hitting the wall and the door.

The brunette screamed in terror as she dove next to the bed.

Ramirez, Malone, and Brown all took cover in the hallway. Cole hurried back to the rest of the team.

Suddenly, another Latino man stepped out of the bathroom. He was shirtless and muscular, with full tattoo sleeves on his arms and a large cursive LK tattoo on his chest with a skull and five-point crown in between the letters. He grabbed the blonde woman by the hair and put an arm around her neck.

"Get the fuck out of here, or this bitch is getting it!" the man barked out.

Malone carefully peeked into the room. He thought he

recognized the man, but couldn't remember his name. The man held a Taurus 627 revolver to the woman's head.

"Freeze! Drop it! Hands on your head!" Malone said.

The man pulled the woman closer and hunched down, using her for cover so Malone could barely see the gunman.

Malone's lips curled over his teeth. "Drop it, asshole!"

"Drop that shit now, or she's getting it right in the head," the gunman said.

Malone kept his gun aimed at the man and felt the trigger with his index finger. He could still only see a partial view of the man's head behind the woman.

The shirtless man said nothing and pressed the revolver harder into the woman's cheek. Tears filled her eyes and she started shaking.

Malone held his gun steady and analyzed the situation. The man's voice wasn't shaky at all. He was holding the gun steady. His eyes were glued on Malone. There was no other choice.

"Okay, okay. I'm putting my gun down," Malone said loudly. He tossed his gun onto the ground and kicked it into the hallway.

The tattooed man fired a burst at Malone, who immediately dove to the hallway floor again for cover. More gunshots rang out behind him. Malone quickly picked up his gun from the ground and out of the corner of his eye saw Brown and Cole nearby with their guns drawn.

Malone stayed on the ground and bumped into something with his leg. It took him a moment to realize it was Ramirez's hand. He had been shot and was lying on the ground.

"No! Shit! No!" Malone screamed as he looked back. Ramirez was still conscious. Barely. He had his palms on his torso and was groaning in pain.

Malone looked around for blood, but there wasn't any. It looked like Ramirez had been protected by his body armor.

Probably just got the wind knocked out of him. Maybe a broken rib or two.

Malone turned back toward the hotel room while staying low in a crouched position. He used his body to cover Ramirez as much as he could.

As he readied himself to fire into the hotel room, three Latin Kings stepped off of the elevator.

Malone could see the men coming down the hallway. Two had handguns and the last man had a sawed-off shotgun. One screamed something out, but Malone couldn't understand what was said.

The three men opened fire, and gunshots filled the air. The earsplitting noise of handguns popping and the boom of a sawed-off shotgun. Malone stayed on top of Ramirez and fired a couple shots at each of the men, going from left to right. The men kept coming.

Brown aimed his Glock at the tattooed man in the hotel room, but he was still using the girl for cover. The man fired a couple shots at Brown, causing him to take cover again.

Back in the hallway, Cole fired a few quick shots at the man with the sawed-off shotgun. Cole shot the man in the right shoulder and he fell over to the ground.

The man with the Glock shot Cole in the leg, causing him to topple over.

Brown moved over to Cole and leaned down, tightening his belt around Cole's leg. "Shit! Fuck! I'm all right, man. Go get those bastards or I will," Cole growled.

Brown nodded and hurried over to stand next to Malone and Ramirez. He crouched down and fired his Glock at the other Latin King holding a handgun. He missed high. Brown fired again and this time his Glock jammed. "Shit!" Brown said.

After firing another quick burst at the men in the hallway, Malone glanced into the open hotel room. The man with the revolver was reloading and the two girls and Junior were nowhere to be found. Malone put in a new clip, turned back, and saw the tattooed man was now approaching the doorway. He flicked his eyes back down the hall. The other two men were getting closer, just a few doors away. Shit. Malone saw a fire extinguisher on the wall. He fired a burst at the fire extinguisher. It exploded with a loud popping sound, spreading cream-colored powder through the air.

"Get the fuck outta here!" Malone barked out to Cole and Brown.

The chemicals burned his nostrils and stung his eyes. The hallway filled with a dusty fog that smelled like an over-chlorinated swimming pool. He fought the urge to wipe his eyes and kept them open.

Malone tugged on Ramirez's arms and picked him up off the ground. He fought for a deeper breath as he tried to carry Ramirez. He couldn't get enough air. Malone gasped and tried again. This time, he grabbed hold of Ramirez and took a wobbly step forward. Then he took another. Once he got to the third step, he had some momentum and kept moving.

Each step felt heavier than the one before it. Malone closed his eyes briefly and kept inching toward the exit. Brown helped Cole get to his feet and started to follow Malone.

Next to the door, Malone saw the red square outline of a fire alarm on the wall and pulled the handle. He knew the sound of the alarm was deafening, but his ears were already ringing from the gunfire. He pulled Ramirez out of the exit and propped him up against a white Dodge pickup. Malone then hurried back inside. Brown and Cole were slowly moving toward the exit. Malone grabbed Brown by the arm and guided them out of the building. Cole took a seat on the ground by Ramirez.

After a few deep breaths, Malone said to Brown, "Call this

shit in. Now!" He pulled his t-shirt up over his nose and rushed back into the cloudy hallway. With his free hand, Malone held his P226 with his finger on the trigger, ready to fire. A hotel door flew open. Malone flinched as a woman in a white bathrobe appeared in the hallway. The woman screamed, but Malone could only see her mouth move. "Chicago Police! Get outta here!" Malone yelled as loud as he could with his mouth covered.

The woman hurried past Malone and ran out the exit. As the fire alarm continued to squeal, Malone tried to down the hallway, but his eyes were so irritated by the chemicals he had to keep closing his eyes. Malone coughed and felt the salty metallic taste building up inside his mouth. He got past most of the chemicals and saw the door to the Latin Kings' hotel room was open. He stopped a few feet before the door and stood against the wall. Then he carefully turned toward the room gun first.

The hotel room was empty. Malone wasn't surprised. They must have left through the lobby. He tried to see down the hallway, but still couldn't see shit. Quickly, he looked down the hall for any other people, but it looked like everyone was already out. He went back outside and caught his breath. Malone sat down on the ground next to Ramirez and breathed deeply.

"Hey. You—okay?" Malone asked.

"Yeah. Hit my vest. Knocked the wind outta me," Ramirez said. "I'm okay, man. Really."

"Good," Malone said, still gasping for air.

"Anyone—else inside?" Ramirez asked.

"Not that I could find." Malone coughed.

"They gotta be close by," Ramirez said. "You take the front entrance, I'll go around the other side."

Malone nodded and carefully got back up to his feet. He scanned the parking lot from one side to the other. Nothing.

The parking lot didn't have many cars in it, other than a few vehicles in the corner. Malone hurried around to the front of the hotel in the parking lot, weaving in between the cars. A family of four dashed out of the hotel. Malone watched the family climb into a blue Dodge minivan. Not the same make and model as Ann's, but close enough to remind him of her. He moved his eyes back to the entrance and saw a few members of the hotel staff come out. A man and two women wearing white dress shirts and black pants stood outside as the fire alarm rang out.

A man in a black polo shirt and khakis scampered into the parking lot talking on a cell phone. The man walked right in front of Malone, nearly running into him. "Watch it," Malone grumbled. The man acted like he didn't hear and then climbed into a shiny red Nissan sedan. Probably a rental car picked up at Midway. Malone scowled as the man pulled out of the parking lot. He turned to the left and saw the three Latin Kings from the hallway storm out of the hotel. Malone aimed his P226 at them. "Freeze! Don't fucking move!" Malone yelled from across the parking lot. The men kept moving, now a couple rows of cars away, and climbed into a black Yukon SUV. Malone ran toward them until the Yukon pulled out of the parking spot and suddenly stopped.

The driver turned the SUV and someone fired a quick burst of gunfire at Malone.

Malone instinctively used a nearby car for cover. Malone knew from the sound it was a handgun, probably a 9mm. As he ducked down, more gunfire came his direction, hitting the front windshield of a green Mustang. Malone fell to the ground completely and crawled to the back of the car. A few more rounds hit the Mustang's hood. Malone fought the urge to immediately return fire. He knew he had to wait. He carefully moved into a crouched position and waited for his opportunity. A break finally came in the gunfire. Malone carefully sat up by the driver's side of the Mustang and fired at the Yukon. He hit the front left tire, deflating it. Then Malone hit the fender and the rest of the clip landed in the driver's door.

The gunman reloaded and fired another burst in Malone's direction.

Malone quickly ducked down again and kept low. He was still feeling lightheaded from breathing in too many chemicals. Malone climbed into the back of a red Ford pickup truck. While the truck bed limited movement, it was a hell of a lot better than nothing. And it gave him another chance to catch his breath. As he laid there, he heard more gunfire fill the air. But this gunfire wasn't coming at him. It was coming from another angle, from further away. Then it popped into his head. Maybe it was Brown. Maybe it was even Cole or Ramirez.

Malone carefully peeked over the side of the truck and saw Brown was crouched by a blue Chevy Blazer for cover. He had opened fire on the Yukon. Ramirez was there too, by the rear bumper of the Blazer, firing at the Yukon from another angle.

Someone in the backseat of the Yukon fired a handgun out the other side of the vehicle at Malone. Malone fired back but missed. Then he shifted his attention back to the driver and fired again. He shot the driver in the head, causing him to fall over onto the steering wheel. The horn blared, and one long continuous note rang out underneath the sound of gunfire. Shots continued, as the man in the passenger seat fired his gun and ignored the sound as he fired the rest of the rounds in the magazine. The passenger then pulled the driver off of the horn, causing the piercing sound to stop. Then he shoved the driver out of the vehicle and his dead body tumbled to the ground.

Malone then recognized the man in the front seat. It was

Junior. He must have snuck around to the car earlier. Behind Junior in the backseat was another Latin King holding a Glock.

Brown sank to the ground and took cover as he reloaded his 9mm with his back to the blue Blazer.

Ramirez fired at the shooter in the back seat, but missed low.

The man in the black coat fired back in Brown's direction, making him take cover behind the car again.

Malone stayed down and crawled on his hands and knees toward the rest of the team.

Once he got to the Blazer, Malone stayed in a crouched position with his back to the taillight. Malone said to Ramirez, "Hey—you good?"

"Yeah. And I'll be even better when we get those pricks," Ramirez said.

Malone nodded his head and kept his eyes focused on the two Latin Kings in front of him. He fired and hit the one to the left.

The man stopped moving and hunched over. Malone flicked his eyes over to Junior.

Junior fired at Malone again.

Malone took cover next to Ramirez and then crouched down low on his knee.

From the ground, Malone fired three more rounds toward Junior. The shots hit the vehicle.

Junior fired back four quick shots, causing both Malone and Ramirez to take cover again.

Malone looked over to Brown and exhaled as he waited.

Suddenly, the sound of more gunfire—from another direction—surprised Malone. Then he realized it was Cole. He was crouched down by the red pickup truck. Cole fired repeatedly and stood up.

"Think Cole just hit that prick in the ear," Malone said to Ramirez.

"Yeah, he ain't gonna be a problem," Ramirez replied.

Malone slowly got up and saw the blood on the side of Junior's head dripping onto his yellow coat. He wasn't dead, but definitely looked out of it. Probably in shock.

The other man in the backseat fired his Glock toward the vehicle almost hitting Brown.

Brown crawled closer to Malone.

"Where the hell's backup?" Malone said.

"Good question," Brown said. "I called it in."

Malone crawled out from under the car and peeked over at the Yukon. The gunman popped up in the backseat and Malone opened fire, hitting the man in the chest. Malone carefully approached the vehicle, Ramirez and Brown right next to him. Once Malone got to the vehicle, he stopped by the rear bumper.

"Get out now! Put your hands on your head," Malone barked. There was no sign of movement inside the SUV. "Last chance. Get out with your hands on your head!" Malone looked over at Ramirez who shrugged slightly. Malone motioned toward Ramirez with hand signals telling him to approach the vehicle on the left side. Malone made his way to the rear door and carefully opened it. Junior was gone. Malone glanced down at the ground. A small blood trail led out of the parking lot toward the street ahead. Malone turned and looked over at Brown. He was pale. Clearly, he hadn't been in a shootout like this before. He wasn't going to be any help.

Malone ran towards the street as fast as he could. His lungs were still burning from the chemicals and his breathing was shallow. He saw Junior turn back and start to run across the street. Malone aimed his P226, but saw the civilians nearby.

"Freeze, asshole! Don't fucking move!"

Junior kept moving, ignoring the command. Malone aimed his weapon at Junior until he saw a mom pushing a stroller nearby. Holstering his weapon, he watched Junior rush across the street and dart down an alley.

Malone slowly walked back toward the rest of the team and looked inside the Yukon. He checked the driver's pockets and found a stack of hundreds banded together. He glanced around to see if anyone was watching him. Nope. The coast was clear. He slipped the cash into the inside pocket of his jacket. Walking back toward the team, he heard the wailing sound of sirens coming toward the hotel. The noise was a cold reminder of death. He felt nauseous and tasted acid in his throat. Malone leaned over and swallowed hard, then spit a few times on the ground and hoped it was over.

He sat down next to Cole who was still in the same place by the blue pickup. It felt good to sit down. He turned toward Cole. "How you doing?" Malone said.

"How you think I'm doing? Feeling like shit. I just got shot, remember?"

"Yeah, I know. Where'd you get it?"

"Shoulder," Cole replied.

"Hurts like hell, don't it? You'll survive though," Malone said.

"You really are an asshole," Cole said.

"Guilty as charged," Malone smiled. "You did good out there, though. Want a cigar?"

"Yeah. Why not?"

Malone helped Cole over to his car and opened the passenger door for him.

"Here you go," Malone said. "Now take a seat. Rest up."

"Thanks," Cole said as he held the cigar up to his lips.

"Keep pressure on your shoulder and try not to bleed all over my car, eh?"

"Fuck you. I'll do what I gotta do."

Malone laughed. "Fair enough. I'm gonna go check on the others. I'll be right back."

Brown was next to Ramirez who was laid out flat on the ground with his eyes closed.

"How's this guy doing over here?" Malone said to Brown.

"Resting at the moment. Seems all right overall. But I think he might have a couple broken ribs," Brown said.

"He'll be back in fighting shape in no time then," Malone replied.

"You know—Ramirez said that wherever you go, a shit storm seems to follow," Brown said.

"Yeah, I get that a lot. Not my fault. It's all these other fucking assholes, you know?"

"You're full of bullshit, Malone," Ramirez said with his eyes closed. "It's your first day back and you got gang members shooting up a hotel and blasting up a parking lot."

"Not my plan for the day, either," Malone replied.

CHAPTER SEVEN

After a fire truck and two ambulances arrived, four CPD police cars appeared in the parking lot. Ramirez and Cole were taken by ambulance to Mercy, and Brown went with them. Malone stayed behind and worked on the paperwork, filling in the details from the incident. Forensics showed up and taped off part of the parking lot and the motel. Malone sat in his car smoking a cigar as he watched the yellow police tape go up. His hand was starting to cramp a bit from the writing. He rolled down the window when he saw an officer, Lauren Tracey, he knew walk out of the hotel. "Hey, Tracey, anything else inside?"

"You didn't see?" Tracey replied.

"See what?"

"Follow me," Tracey said.

Malone put out his cigar and followed Tracey back into the hotel and onto the elevator. On the second floor, Tracey turned left and stopped in the hallway and held up the police tape for Malone. Inside the room were the two prostitutes from earlier. One was lying on the floor and the other on the bed. Both were nude and lifeless.

"Found five dead prostitutes in all. Looks like overdoses. We also found evidence of heroin use."

"What? Where were the rest?" Malone asked.

"Three more on the next floor. Hotel staff found them when they were evacuating."

"Motherfucker," Malone said as he gasped for air. "Anything else?"

"Only a couple witnesses on this floor. A flight attendant and an accountant. Both didn't see much. Got a few casings in the hotel room and in the hallway. A blood trail that led to the parking lot, but you know about that. That's about it," Tracey said. The two officers headed back outside.

"Any leftover drugs?"

"Some trace amounts. Lab results will take some time."

"Yeah," Malone said, "Have 'em call me with whatever they find."

"Sure thing," Tracey replied.

After finishing the paperwork, Malone sat alone in his car. Ramirez and Cole would be okay, but this was still all too familiar.

Someone knocked on the window. It was Tracey again. He rolled the window down. "What's up? I thought you left."

"You going over to Mercy?" Tracey asked.

"No, I can't. I..." Malone's voice trailed off.

"Come on. I'll head over there with you."

"I can't. Really." Malone looked ahead and avoided eye contact with Tracey.

"Just for a couple minutes. Show up, say hello, and leave. That's it," Tracey said.

"I hear you. But I gotta go. I can't." Malone put his key into the car's ignition.

"Just make it really goddamn quick."

"No. I can't. Not again. Not now." Malone turned the key and shifted the car into drive.

"Understood. See you later," Tracey said.

Malone hoped he could get his shit together on the way back to Ann's, but he was exhausted. It'd been a long fucking day, and he'd been going on sheer adrenaline. He tapped his hands on the steering wheel as he pulled up in front of Ann's house and put the car into park.

He remembered the first time he saw the house five years ago. Ann was sitting next to him in the passenger seat of an old, blue Honda Civic they had before they owned a minivan. She was six months pregnant and craved pickles all the time. Pickles for breakfast, pickles for lunch, pickles for dinner. It was like it was both yesterday and a lifetime ago.

Malone climbed out of his car and walked to the front door. Ever since moving out, he wondered if he should knock or just enter. He fought the urge to knock every time and Ann never really told him. Since she was expecting him, he just went in. He saw James inside on the living room floor watching cartoons. He sprung up and ran toward Malone, jumping into Malone's arms.

"Dad! You're back!"

"Hey. I'm here. Sorry I had to run earlier. How're you doing?"

Malone put James down on the couch.

"I'm great. Mom let me stay up late and watch some Road Runner cartoons!"

"Nice. That ol' coyote doesn't have a chance, does he?"

"Nope! He's never gonna get 'im," James said with a smile.

"Sorry I had to run earlier," Malone said to Ann.

"It's all right. Are you okay? You look like a mess."

"Oh yeah. I should go shower and change out of these clothes."

"What happened?"

"Fire extinguisher."

"Did someone spray you? It looks like it's even in your hair."

"Something like that. I'll be fast. Just give me a few minutes."

Malone took a quick shower and changed into a t-shirt and some shorts.

"I threw those clothes in the washer," Malone said as he walked into the living room.

"Are you hungry? I know there's some leftovers in the fridge…"

"Yeah, I'm starved. Thanks." Malone went and made a plate and came back to the living room. He took a bite of the pasta. It was ice cold, but he gulped it down.

"You doing any fun projects in school?" Malone asked.

"Miss Tucker had us do a new art project. Wanna see it?"

"Of *course* I do," Malone replied. "Where is it?"

"I'll get it!" James got up from the couch and ran into the kitchen. James returned proudly holding a drawing of a snowman wearing a blue hat and a red scarf standing on what looked like an orange surfboard.

Malone smiled. "Nice! Is he snowboarding down the hill?"

"Yep. He sure is!"

"I like it. And you did a good job with those colors too. Very nice!"

"You can keep it, if you want."

"Can we hang it up on the fridge?"

"Sure!"

Malone and James took the picture back to the kitchen.

"I found a great spot for it!" James pointed to the one empty space on the refrigerator.

"Yeah, that's great." Malone put a small red ladybug magnet on the page to hold it up.

"That's perfect! Mom, you gotta see this," James said.

Ann came into the kitchen. "Oh, yeah. That looks great there. Nice job."

Malone went back to the living room and took another bite of pasta.

"Hey, Dad?"

"Yes, pal?"

"Who's the strongest superhero you know?"

"I dunno," Malone rubbed his chin. "I'd say It's probably a toss up between Mom and Wonder Woman."

Ann smiled.

"Really? Mom always wants you to open jars."

Malone laughed and then covered it up with his hand. "Well, jars don't count," Malone said.

"I thought you'd say Superman or the Hulk."

"You think those are the strongest?"

"Yep."

"I think I'd still vote for Mom."

"Gee, thanks. You saying I'm scary?" Ann said.

"No, no. Not scary. Just strong. It's a compliment," Malone said with a smile.

"Oh really?" Ann said in a serious tone.

"Oh yeah. You know I'm just joking."

Ann smiled and laughed. "I got you so good there," she said as she took the empty plate back to the kitchen. "How about we have that dessert?"

"Yeah!" James said.

Ann pulled a white box out of the freezer.

Malone loaded the dinner plates into the dishwasher.

"You trying to earn some brownie points?"

"Who me?" Malone said with a smirk.

"It may be working. Anything else happen today?"

"I had to—uh—talk to the shrink earlier today. They obviously cleared me for field duty."

"Oh yeah?" Ann said. She pulled a slice of ice cream cake out of the box and put it on a small white plate.

"Yeah. I think it went pretty well."

Ann bit her lip as she plated another slice. "You're saying that—that—you found therapy helpful?"

"I suppose I am. Not saying I loved it at first. New supervisor sprung it on me outta nowhere."

"That sounds more like it. Don't bullshit me, or I'll have to kick your ass," Ann whispered in Malone's ear. She then put a piece of cake on another plate.

"Believe me, I know it," Malone replied with a laugh.

Malone winked at Ann as he took the plate from her hand.

"You ain't gonna believe this. Look at what Mom picked out for dessert," Malone said. He set the plate of ice cream cake down on the table.

James had a wide smile on his face.

"Looks really good, doesn't it?" Malone said.

"Sure does! Can I have some now?" James had the spoon in his hand hovering over the plate.

"You sure can."

James crammed his spoon into the ice cream cake and stuffed a bite into his mouth.

"I think someone is enjoying himself over here," Malone said. He pointed at James with his mouthful.

"This is really, really good," James said. His voice was muffled by a mouthful of dessert.

"What can I say, Mom has good taste," Ann replied.

Malone took a bite and smiled.

"Do you want to stay and watch a movie together?" Ann asked.

"I'd love to. Not sure how long I'll stay awake though," Malone said.

"It's okay if you fall asleep."

"You sure?" Malone asked.

"Mmm-hmm," Ann said, taking her first bite of dessert.

"Okay then. Let's do it."

Malone turned to James. "What do you wanna watch?"

"How about something *funny*?"

"You mean Roadrunner cartoons, don't you?"

"Uh-huh." James said with a smile. He ate the last bite of his dessert.

Malone laughed. "Okay, sure."

After finishing dessert, all three piled on the couch. Malone to the right, Ann to the left and James in between them. A couple minutes into the first cartoon, Malone was fast asleep laying close to James's shoulder.

James nudged him with his arm, but it didn't wake Malone.

Ann chuckled. "It's okay, just let Dad sleep for a minute."

Twenty minutes later, Malone woke up. He wasn't sure how long he'd been sleeping.

"Have a nice nap?" Ann asked.

"No, no. I was just resting my eyes for a little bit," Malone said with a yawn.

"You were snoring in my ear, Dad," James said.

"You sure that was me?" Malone said with a laugh.

"Dad, you sound like a grizzly bear!"

"Sorry, pal. I'm awake now. Did that coyote fall off the cliff a few times already?"

"Yep. He sure did. He's silly!"

Malone smiled as he soaked up the moment. He hadn't sat on the couch with his family in over six months, let alone napped next to them.

Ann looked up at the clock. "Buddy, you gotta get to bed. It's past your bedtime."

"Come on, Mom, just one more episode?"

"No, you gotta go to bed, pal. It's time," Malone said with a slight yawn.

"I think it's time for Dad to go to bed too," Ann said.

Malone nodded slightly in agreement and chuckled.

"Go brush your teeth, and put on your pajamas," Ann said to James.

"Dad, will you tuck me in?"

"Sure, pal. You bet."

James hurried upstairs.

Malone yawned again and went upstairs following James to his room. James hopped into his bed and Malone tucked him in. His room hadn't changed much since Malone moved out six months ago. Sure, there were a few new toys. A dinosaur here and a monster truck there, but otherwise, everything looked the same.

James was already fast asleep. Malone watched James sleep for a moment and then went back downstairs. He sat down next to Ann on the couch.

"I know you've had a helluva day," Ann said. "You're too tired to drive. Stay here. Go to bed. It's totally fine."

"Okay. Where do you want me to sleep?" Malone asked, while he yawned again.

"Your call."

"Okay, how about the couch? I don't want to keep you awake with my snoring."

"Believe me, I'm quite used to it. Might have even missed it." Ann's eyes widened and she put her right hand in her auburn hair.

"Yeah, right," Malone smiled.

"Let me get you some sheets and a pillow."

Ann went upstairs to the linen closet. She found a blue pillow, some fresh white sheets, and a tan blanket. When she got back downstairs, she found Malone stretched out on the couch fast asleep. She stood there for a moment watching him and then covered him with the blanket. She sat down by his feet and the sound of Malone snoring was somehow comforting.

A couple hours later, Malone woke up in the dark and sat up on the couch. He was covered in sweat and didn't know where he was until a car drove by, the headlights revealing the photos on the wall. The heart palpitations were back again. He knew he was alone, but it felt like someone was watching him. Like someone knew what he was doing and they wanted him dead.

Malone rose to his feet and got a glass of water. He stood by the kitchen sink as he waited to feel better and thought of James playing in the backyard. He waited for the pounding to lessen. Suddenly, a loud bang came from outside close to the house. The glass slipped out of his hand and landed on the side of the sink. It shattered, sending water and pieces of glass flying all over.

"Shit!" Malone screamed quickly as the cold water and glass splashed on his arms, chest, and legs. He shook his head in disgust. Then he cursed again under his breath as he took some paper towels off of the counter.

Ann hurried down the stairs and into the kitchen.

Malone flinched when he saw her.

"What happened? Are you all right?" Ann said. She had wide eyes and was visibly shaken.

"Some noise outside spooked me, and I dropped my glass," Malone said with a shrug.

"Are you okay?"

"Yeah, I'm okay."

"It was probably a cat or a raccoon in the trash," Ann said. She took a deep breath as she saw the mess on the floor and the blood on Malone's hand.

"You're bleeding a bit. You sure you're okay?"

Malone looked down at his left hand. "Oh, that's just a

scratch. I guess I got that picking up the glass. Where'd you put the broom?"

"In the corner of the pantry."

"Okay, I wouldn't walk over here. There's glass every-where." Malone carefully walked over to the pantry.

"Let me get you a Band-Aid."

"Sure."

Ann had a furrowed brow and bite her lip as she searched in a drawer.

"Have you been up long?"

Ann handed Malone the bandage.

"No. I just needed a drink of water. That's all," Malone swept the glass into a pile with the broom.

"Let me get that. Rest your hand." Ann swept up the glass on the floor and dumped it into the trash can.

"I think that's most of it," Ann said.

"Yeah. Thanks. Good—good night."

"Good night," Malone said as he watched her go up the stairs.

"Hey, Ann?"

Ann turned around on the stairs. "Yeah?"

"Can I sleep in bed with you? That couch ain't doing me any favors."

"Sure. As long as you behave yourself."

"You know me," Malone said as he climbed the stairs.

"Yeah, that's the problem," Ann said. "Then again, I may not say no."

Ann climbed into bed on the right and Malone laid down on the left side. Ann turned and kissed Malone. Malone pulled her closer and put his arms around Ann. They continued to kiss. Malone pulled away slightly.

"Don't stop yet," Ann said, and kissed him again. Malone reached over and turned off the light.

The next morning, James came running into the bedroom. Malone woke up and rubbed his eyes.

"Hey bud," Malone said with a yawn.

"Dad, I'm hungry. How about some breakfast?"

"What time is it?" Malone yawned again.

Ann stirred in the bed.

"It's already seven, Dad!"

"Since when'd he stop sleeping in?" Malone said.

"Past few months." Ann said in a muffled voice.

"I see." Malone turned back to James. "Yeah, we can have some breakfast. How does cereal sound?"

"Great." James smiled widely.

"Okay, pal. You got it. Why don't you meet me downstairs, okay?"

James ran off.

Malone turned back to Ann who was now sitting up in bed. "Any idea where my boxers are?" Malone asked.

"Not sure," Ann said as she looked under the covers and then under the bed. "Here you go," she said as she tossed them at Malone.

"Thanks," Malone said. He got out of bed and slipped the boxers on. After he finished getting dressed, he came downstairs.

James was already sitting at the dining room table and Malone grabbed two bowls, spoons, milk, and two boxes of cereal.

"What do you think—Apple Jacks or Golden Grahams?"

"Apple Jacks for me!"

"You got it," Malone said. He poured the cereal into the bowl and then added milk.

"I think I'm going to have Golden Grahams mixed with Apple Jacks."

"That's silly," James said with a laugh.

"It can be fun being silly."

Malone made a goofy face as he poured the Golden Grahams into his bowl.

"You gonna add the Apple Jacks now?" James said as he stared at Malone's bowl of cereal.

"Yep. Are you ready? Oh, wait a minute. Close your eyes!"

"Why?"

"Just do it," Malone insisted.

James closed his eyes.

Malone pulled the box of Lucky Charms out of the pantry. Then he put Lucky Charms and Apple Jacks on top of the other cereal in the shape of a smile.

"Okay, open 'em!"

James grinned as he admired his cereal. "Dad, you're so silly!"

Ann walked into the room and Malone quickly took a bite of his cereal. "What's going on in here?" Ann asked in a semi-serious tone.

Malone realized that tone. It was the one she used when she was teaching.

"Nothing," Malone said with a mouthful of cereal. He leaned over and put his arms around his bowl of cereal.

Ann looked over at James. "Tell me—what's going on?"

James tried to hold in his chuckle but it quickly turned into a full laugh. "Dad mixed all of the cereal together," James said.

"Who me?" Malone swallowed the rest of his bite.

"Golden Grahams and Apple Jacks, eh?" Ann said.

"Might be some Lucky Charms in there, too," Malone replied.

"Want some, Mom?" James said with a wide grin.

"I think I'll pass," Ann replied.

"Don't knock it 'til you've tried it," Malone replied.

James continued to laugh.

"Really, that's okay."

"More for us then," Malone said to James.

"I—pulled some of your clothes out for you." Ann sat a small stack of clothes down on an empty chair next to Malone.

Thanks," Malone said as picked them up. It was a pair of jeans, a t-shirt, a solid navy blue button-down shirt, some socks, and underwear all neatly stacked in a pile. "This is great. I'm gonna go get dressed. If you change your mind, you're welcome to some of my wonderful cereal."

"Right. Thanks," Ann said as poured water into the coffeemaker.

Malone took a quick shower and got dressed. When he came downstairs, he found James sitting by himself crying at the table.

"Hey, pal. What's wrong?"

"Mom said you gotta go to work."

"Yeah, I do. Don't you have school today too?"

"Yeah. I don't wanna go. I wanna stay home with you."

"I'll tell you what... let's do something fun tonight."

"Really? Like what?"

"It's a surprise."

"Come on Dad, tell me more than that!"

"A fun surprise. I need to talk to Mom about it."

James stared down at the kitchen tile and continued to pout. Finally, he whispered, "Okay, fine."

"Hey—" Malone put his hand on James's shoulder. "It'll be fun. I mean it."

It was impossible not to think back to the many times he had to cancel plans before. Soccer games missed for stake-outs. Trips to the zoo missed because of a hangover. Birthday parties missed because of drug busts. He didn't blame James for thinking it wasn't going to happen.

Ann came back into the room wearing dark jeans, a purple sweater, and a brown leather coat. Malone noticed she was wearing a pair of diamond earrings that he had given her for their tenth anniversary.

"You look really nice," Malone said, "those earrings look great on you."

Ann smiled and said, "Thanks. Today just felt like a great day to wear them."

"We need to get going," Ann said to James, "so please put on your shoes and coat."

Malone got up and pulled the white jewelry box out of the inside pocket of his leather jacket. James started to cram his feet into his still-tied sneakers. "Need some help?" Malone asked.

"No, I got it," James said as he pulled the shoe on. "See?"

"Very good. James, why don't you grab your backpack and meet us at the car?" Malone said.

Malone waited until he was gone and held out the jewelry box to Ann.

"Really?" Ann said with wide eyes.

Malone nodded.

Ann opened the box and saw the silver bracket. "It's beautiful. Thanks." Ann leaned over and kissed Malone on the cheek.

"You're welcome."

"What was he crying about earlier?" Ann asked as she admired the bracelet on her wrist.

"Me going to work. I told him I'd like to surprise him tonight. Something really fun. Please tell me you don't already have plans tonight."

"No. No plans. That sounds nice. Maybe take him to one of those kid's indoor playground places? There's a trampoline park in Ravenswood."

"That's perfect. Maybe we can grab dinner together afterwards? Eating before jumping on a trampoline could be a problem," Malone said.

Ann laughed. "Good point. Yeah, that sounds great."

Malone smiled at Ann and then went outside by James, who was staring at the ground. "Okay, pal, we've got a serious surprise planned out for later."

James didn't look up.

"Have a great day, pal. We're gonna have some fun later." Malone gave James a hug.

Ann walked up behind them. "Have a great day at work."

"Yeah, you too."

Malone started walking down the street toward his car. Last night, all of the nearby parking spots were gone. Ann's minivan was also parked on the street. He froze. On the driver's door was a large five-point crown and the letters ADR underneath. A common tag from the Latin Kings. The letters ADR stood for "amor de rey" which meant love of the king in English.

He immediately felt his heart beating hard in his chest and tightened his jaw. Ann's mouth opened wide in disbelief. He then noticed the tires were flat on the driver's side.

"Mom, what's that?" James said. Ann reached down and grabbed James.

"It's just some goofy kids tagging. I'll—uh—get this taken care of," Malone said.

"Okay, fine," Ann said.

"These fuckers are out of control," Malone mumbled to himself.

"Dad can take you to school today," Ann said to James.

"Okay!"

"I'll—uh—take you to work too, of course," Malone replied. "And I'll get that fixed as soon as possible."

"I'll get his car seat," Ann said quietly. "Where's your car?"

"Had to park down the block. I'll go get it."

Malone hurried to his car and was relieved that it did not have any gang tags on it and that it had four inflated tires. He cleared some trash and fast food wrappers off of the passenger seat and then leaned back to grab a hoodie, hat, and gloves from the backseat. He popped the trunk and spotted the bolt cutters, then thought of the money at the storage unit. It also reminded him that he needed to check on Sarah. He covered the bolt cutters with his hoodie and shut the trunk.

Ann had already put the car seat in the car and James was sitting in it. Ann was in the passenger seat.

"Sorry it's so messy in here. A lot of stakeouts, you know."

Ann didn't reply. She blew her nose in a tissue.

Malone exhaled loudly. "I'm sorry about all that stuff. Been a crazy morning."

"Yeah," Ann replied. "We better hurry. Don't want to be late."

"Right."

A few turns later, they were already stuck in traffic. Malone sighed again as he looked at all of the cars in front of him, none of them moving.

"What if I uh—turned on the siren?"

James perked up. "Yeah Dad, do that!"

Malone looked over at Ann.

"That okay with you?"

"I—guess—" Ann said, disgustedly.

Malone flipped on the siren and the cars ahead moved to the side of the road. Soon the car was cruising down the road.

Ann looked back at James, who had a big grin on his face and couldn't help but smile too. "Somebody's loving this."

"I'm sure he is," Malone said. This was the first time the three of them had been together outside of the house in quite a while. Malone turned the siren off as the car approached James's preschool.

"Look at that, you're not even late," Malone said as he saw some other kids lined up outside the school.

"That was pretty good," Ann said.

"Can we do that again?" James said.

"Sorry, pal, it's time for school," Malone said with a chuckle. "Have a good day. I love you."

"Yeah. Thanks Dad!"

James got out of the car and walked into the school.

"And just like that, he forgot all about Mom," Ann said.

"Nah. He was just excited about the siren."

"Yeah. Look, I dunno what the hell happened with the car, but that scared the shit out of me."

"Yeah. I get it. I really think it was just some new gang members trying to get street cred."

"I dunno. This place just ain't the same anymore."

"I'll get your door fixed and some new tires for you. We can install a security camera too right by the house."

"An even better idea is moving to a nicer area," Ann said.

"Hard to move on a cop's salary, you know? Especially with the economy right now," Malone said.

"You know, you're not the *only* one working," Ann said.

"You're right. I'm sorry."

Ann didn't answer.

"Do you—uh—got any showings today?"

"Surprisingly, no. But I've got some admin work to do. I have three showings tomorrow."

"Remind me where your office is?"

"In Willis Tower."

"Great location there," Malone said as he turned onto I-90 North.

"Yeah, it's nice. My boss is pretty great."

The two sat in silence for a few minutes as Malone drove down the interstate. Malone looked over at Ann briefly and flicked his eyes back to the road. He noticed she was staring at him.

"What?" Malone asked.

"Tell me something. You really quit drinking?"

"Yeah. Not a drop. After being laid up in the hospital and damn near dying, I'm done." Malone checked the mirrors and switched lanes.

"You going to meetings?" Ann asked as she flipped down the visor and checked her makeup in the mirror.

"No, I haven't. A little worried what happens if that gets out."

"They call it Alcoholics Anonymous for a reason, right? You should go."

"I want to. But..." Malone bit his lip.

Ann turned to look at Malone. "But what?"

Malone took a deep breath. "I dunno. Maybe just talking to a counselor would be better. Less worry about the possible backlash. Maybe I can continue to talk to Isley."

"Is that who you spoke with yesterday?"

"Yeah. It went okay. I can try talking to her again." He took the exit which looped around to South Wacker Drive and came to a stop in front of Willis Tower.

"That's a good idea."

"Yeah."

"You know, I used to think you'd never change. Maybe you can after all," Ann said with a smile as she got out of the car.

Malone smiled back. "I'm full of surprises. I'll pick you up tonight. Just let me know when."

"That'd be great. Oh, I forgot to tell you, James gets out at 2:30 today."

"Oh. I'll uh—I'll figure something out. Maybe I can skip lunch and take the afternoon off," Malone said.

"I really appreciate it," Ann said.

Malone glanced down at his phone before he put the car in drive. One missed call from Mitchell. He lit a cigar before he called her back.

"Where the hell are you?" Mitchell said.

"Had some car troubles. On my way right now to the office."

"No, get your ass over here to Mercy Hospital. I'm here now with the rest of the team."

"Yeah. Okay. I'm on my way." Malone hung up and growled out loud.

CHAPTER EIGHT

The idea of going back to the hospital made Malone want to throw up. The same nightmare was happening again and again. More shootings. More death. Everywhere he looked, he saw bad memories full of ghosts that wouldn't leave. Malone pulled up in front of the hospital and rubbed his temples with his fingers. He could do this. He had to. There was no other choice, or the team would think he wasn't supportive and didn't care. It was part of being a cop. His stomach continued to churn fast. He ignored the feeling and flung the door open and got out of the car. As he moved his feet onto the asphalt, his stomach tightened even more. He leaned over and threw up in front of an ambulance, barely missing the front bumper. The sight of the vomit on the ground made him look away. The bitter taste of acid in his mouth lingered. He leaned over again and spat on the ground.

Malone realized that some vomit was on the sleeve of his leather jacket. *Shit.* He looked back at his Chevy and remembered the time Max threw up on his leather jacket right in the very same parking lot. They had spent all night drinking after his nephew Andrew died from an overdose. It felt like yesterday. He then threw up again. His stomach muscles ached now, and the bitter taste remained in his mouth. Malone wiped his mouth with the back of his hand. Then he rifled through his jacket pockets and found an old receipt and wiped his hands on it.

He felt a little better now with an empty stomach, but his nerves were shot. He tossed the receipt into the trashcan as he walked into the hospital.

Malone saw Mitchell by the hospital entrance, smoking a cigarette.

"Where the hell have you been? Brown said he called you an hour ago."

"Sorry. Must have missed his call. Car trouble. What's going on?"

Mitchell held the cigarette up to her lips and took a long drag. Then she crushed the cigarette under the heel of her black shoe. "Listen to me. Cops show up for other cops. A fellow officer goes down, you fucking show up."

Malone nodded.

"Follow me," she said as she looked Malone up and down. "Damn. You look like shit, Malone."

"Long night."

Once inside, Mitchell led Malone to the vending machines and stopped in front of the coffee machine.

As the coffee streamed down into the cup, she frowned for a moment and then turned towards Malone. "Are you hungover? You seem out of it. I'll send your ass packing."

"No. Not a fucking drop. Just rough night. Rough morning too. I had to drop of my kid off at school and wife at work. That's why I'm late."

"Look, if you're gonna be late, you need to let someone know. My command, my rules. Got it?"

"Yeah, I get it. Are we done here?"

"No, there's something else." Mitchell set her coffee down

on the gray table and crossed her arms. "Cole will be out a few days and is already home. Ramirez has some bruised ribs and is still here in his room."

"Shit. Is Ramirez okay now?"

"Yeah. He just needs to lay low for a day or two."

"I see," Malone said.

"Now, I got you and Brown in office today. Cole will be back tomorrow. What I wanna know is if you can keep your shit together. Can I trust you to follow up on this incident? If not, I'll just replace you right now." Mitchell carefully picked up her coffee and slowly took a sip.

"Yeah. I'll be fine. I got this," Malone replied.

"Good. I'm putting Brown in charge until Ramirez is back. That gonna be a problem?"

"Nope. I just got back. Whatever you need, you got it."

Mitchell sized up Malone and looked him directly in the eye. "Okay. Keep me in the loop. I find out you're doing your own thing and just telling me what I wanna hear, I'm going for your fucking badge, you hear me?"

"Understood. Like I said, I ain't gonna be a problem."

"You sure about that? Where's your fucking report from last night?"

"I've got it. Must have left it in my car. I'll have it on your desk today."

"Damn right. I'll see about getting a few more guys sent to Vice."

"Maybe ask Carver? He might be able to cash in a favor or something."

Mitchell scowled back at Malone. "When I want your advice, I'll ask for it."

"Sorry. Just trying to help."

"When did you become such a boy scout?"

"This shit's a lot bigger than me. I seriously just wanna help. You want me to go back to HQ?"

"Yeah. Help Brown with the case. Track down the assholes who shot up the Marriott and see how it's all tied to prostitution."

"Right. You—"

Mitchell pulled her phone out of her pocket and answered it. She waved toward him and mouthed the word "go."

Malone nodded and walked out of the break room. He saw Brown in the lobby and approached him. "How's Ramirez doing?"

"He's stable and quite medicated," Brown said.

"I see," Malone replied. Malone's eyes flicked down the hallway. This was the same part of the hospital where he stayed just a few weeks ago. A sharp pain built up in Malone's stomach. A twisting ache that made him think his insides were going to explode. Malone wanted to leave, now. To get the hell out of there and never come back. But he remembered how Ramirez stayed in his room when he was there. He had to do it, just for a minute. He gritted his teeth and ignored everything inside of him that wanted to run out of the building.

"Hey," Malone said quietly, "can you show me to his room?"

"Did you not hear me? We gotta get back to the station," Brown said.

"Just for a minute. Where's his room?"

Brown led Malone down the hallway.

If Malone had anything left in his stomach, he would've vomited again, right in the middle of the hallway.

They passed the first few rooms in the middle of the hallway.

No. Malone watched as Brown's feet kept moving forward. *Not that room.*

They continued to move forward.

No, not that fucking room.

Brown stopped at the end of the hallway and pointed towards the room on the left. Malone exhaled. Across the hallway to the right, he knew the room all too well. That was where his former teammate Leo died after being shot.

Malone refocused his thoughts and reminded himself that he couldn't stay long. That thought gave him comfort. He slowly entered the room and was glad to see Carver sitting next to a sleeping Ramirez.

"Hey," Malone said quietly. He stopped at the foot of the bed.

"Hey," Carver replied.

"How's he doing?"

"He's been asleep. Looks like he's gonna be okay."

"That's good."

Carver yawned. Malone noticed his eyes were bloodshot. He'd probably been up all night. "Maybe you should get some rest too," Malone said. "Been here a while?"

"A while," Carver rubbed his eyes.

"We're heading back to headquarters. Need a lift?"

"I'm good. Thanks," Carver said. "Think I'm gonna head out now that you're here." He slowly rose from his chair and stretched his arms out over his head.

"I'm just gonna stay—stay here for a minute," Malone said. "He was there for me. I wanna be there for him too."

Carver nodded his head and left. On the way out, Carver said to Brown, "Don't let him stay here too long."

"Yes, sir," Brown said.

As Malone sat next to the hospital bed, the beeping sound of the medical equipment made him want to cover his ears with his hands and close his eyes. Death was surrounding him, an ever-present shadow that followed him everywhere.

Malone opened his eyes and saw that Ramirez was awake. His lips were moving, and he was whispering something.

"What's that?" Malone leaned closer.

"Fourth floor," Ramirez whispered.

"What? Fourth floor? What about the fourth floor?"

"Proctology. That's where the assholes go. Proctology's on fourth floor," Ramirez said in a louder voice. He then smiled at Malone.

"Good to see you too," Malone said with a laugh. "How you feeling?"

"Not bad. These painkillers got me feeling pretty good."

"Good? You seem a little fucking loopy," Malone shot back.

"Maybe a little bit, Sergeant Asshole."

"Well, at least you got my title right," Malone said.

Ramirez laughed.

"Heard you're gonna be out for a couple days."

Ramirez shrugged.

"Ain't nothing wrong with getting paid to sit on your ass. Just like one of the bosses, right?"

Ramirez laughed really loud. "Fuck yeah. Sounds like a good plan ta' me." Ramirez slurred his words.

"I'm gonna let you get some rest, okay?"

"Okay, man. Ain't nothin' you can do here. Go out and get the bad guys."

Malone smiled. Ramirez was more like him than he realized, at least when he was heavily medicated.

"Okay, deal. Rest up, sleeping beauty."

CHAPTER NINE

Someone had changed the sign on the door from Gang Task Force to Vice. Seeing the change made Malone feel both irritated and relieved at the same time. He tried to ignore the sensation and followed Brown into the office.

Brown sat down at his desk and logged into his computer.

"What's the—uh—plan?" Malone asked as he sat down.

"What do you mean?" Brown replied.

"Mitchell said you're in charge."

"Oh yeah?" Brown said.

"Yeah. So, what do you want me to do?"

"Hmm. Well..." Brown's voice trailed off. Malone crossed his arms as he waited. Brown didn't say anything else.

"We got any intel on any of these assholes from yesterday?" Malone blurted.

"I got names and photos there," Brown replied. He motioned toward the wall.

Malone cupped his hand over his mouth and felt the stubble on his face. He stood in front of the faces tacked to the wall and stared at the photos for a moment. Angel Lopez.

Diego Gonzalez. Junior Garcia. Victor Salazar. So many faces with cold eyes. Malone exhaled and looked back over at Brown. "What kind of priors did we have on these guys?"

"Theft, B and E, possession, aggravated assault, armed robbery, you name it."

"Did we get any video footage from the hotel?" Malone said.

"Yes, we did. I sent it to Mitchell."

"Oh yeah?" Malone replied.

"Yeah. She likes to be hands-on."

"I see," Malone said. "You watch it?"

"Not yet. She said there wasn't much there."

"Share that footage with me." Malone sat back down and logged onto his computer. While he waited, he picked up an old baseball off of the desk and lightly tossed it in the air and caught it.

"Okay. You should have it now," Brown said.

Malone opened the file Brown sent over and a video popped up on the screen. He quickly scrolled through the video and watched the people dance across the screen in the hotel hallway. Half of the footage all he could see was the powder in the air from the fire extinguisher. "This it? Nothing else from the lobby or the parking lot?" Malone shifted in his seat.

"That's all we received," Brown said.

"All right." Malone watched the video play. He couldn't find much footage of the Latin Kings. Nothing with Ramirez getting shot either.

He scowled as he continued to watch the screen. "Can you double check that we didn't get anything else?"

"Yeah. Doing that right now." Brown pushed back his glasses on his nose and then bounced his eyes back to the computer screen. "Yeah, I sent you everything."

"Shit! This is fucking useless!" He scrolled through the video again and stopped once he saw the Latin Kings coming down the hallway and then disappear out of frame.

Malone sighed while he continued to rewatch the video. "There's gotta be something more. Can you hit up the Marriott again? They gotta have *something* from the parking lot."

"Yeah. I'll do that," Brown said, "you stay here."

"Did we run the plates on the vehicle? That black Yukon?" Malone asked.

"I ran it. Nothing there. Car was clean. Was actually a rental."

"Talk to the rental agency?"

"Not yet." Brown sat back down at his desk.

"Why don't I do that?"

"Okay, I'll send you that info right now." Brown typed on the keyboard.

A message popped up in the corner of Malone's screen. "Got it."

The address was for the Hertz Car Rental on 5259 South Archer Avenue. Malone knew the place. It was right by Midway airport and about a half mile down the road from the Starbucks and muffler shop where Ramirez did his stake out the night before.

"I'll go back over to the Marriott. Like you said, there has to be more there," Brown said as he left.

"Agreed," Malone said.

Malone zipped through the video file again and again. After about an hour, he looked at his watch. It was 11:30 now. James would get out of school at 2:30. He called the number for Hertz Car Rental and no one picked up. He decided to go check it out in person.

He pulled into Ducky's Car Wash across the street from

the rental car lot and dropped a few quarters into the coin-operated vacuum, then held the vacuum on the car's floor mat, sucking up crumbs and small pieces of trash on the floor. Across the street, he could see the Hertz Car Rental. The cars were surrounded by a large black gate and thick trees and bushes. There wasn't much to see.

As the vacuum shut off, Malone got back into his Impala and turned down South Komar Avenue, which ran right next to the Hertz parking lot. Malone found the entrance and pulled in and parked. There were rows and rows of cars and a rectangle-shaped gray building in the middle of the parking lot. He stayed in his car, watching and waiting.

No one was around, so Malone approached the building. He saw one young man with slicked back hair leave the building. He was wearing a white polo and khakis. The man hurried over to a silver Camry, then pulled out of the lot. Malone entered the building. Once inside, he flashed his police badge and asked to talk to the manager. "I'm afraid the manager just left," a young girl with curly red hair said.

"Okay. Maybe you can help me? I'm with the Chicago Police. I have a car that was involved in a crime from this location." Malone handed over the small sheet of paper with the make, model, and license plate number for the car.

"I'm afraid I can't help you with this. You'll have to wait to talk to the manager."

Malone leaned forward and said calmly but confidently, "Ma'am, I'm a police officer. I know you can help me with this. All I need is a name and whatever info you have. Then I'll be on my way."

The girl sighed, glanced down at the paper, and then pounded the keyboard in front of her. She then exhaled again as she punched in a few more keystrokes.

"I don't see anything."

"You're sure? Nothing at all?" Malone blurted out.

The girl shook her head no as she continued to look at the screen. "Maybe the manager can help you when he gets back?"

"Yeah, sure. That's fine. Let me give you my card," Malone said as he looked for a business card in his jacket pocket. He felt the wad of cash that he took yesterday and then found the card. "Here you go. Thanks for all of your help," Malone said as he handed it over.

The girl took the business card, rolled her eyes at Malone and then looked back at the computer screen.

Malone sighed as he got back into his car. He wasn't going to get anything from this girl. The clock on the dashboard read 12:05. He could just take lunch now. He stopped at Paco's Tacos and picked up some tacos. As he walked back to his car, he decided to take some of the food to his sister, Sarah. She had stopped by the hospital briefly right before he was released. Other than that, he hadn't seen her.

Malone pulled up in front of sister's small townhouse. Sarah's was a corner unit and had a red brick exterior. Malone wanted to smoke a cigar before going inside, but knew he didn't have time. He went to the dark brown door and knocked but no one answered.

After a couple minutes, Malone went around to the back door. He tested the door and it was open. Malone shook his head in disgust as he stepped into the kitchen. Once inside, he found a mountain of dirty dishes next to a stack of pizza boxes and take out containers. He sat down the bag of tacos, picked up a vodka bottle, and felt the weight of the liquid swishing around inside. He thought about holding it up to his lips and how it would taste. Instead, he walked over to the sink, poured the contents of the bottle down the drain, and tossed the empty bottle into the trash.

Dark curtains were closed in the front of the house and cast the entire living room in a gray light. Malone found Sarah passed out on the couch. Malone knocked over a vodka bottle and the sound woke her.

"Wha? W—who is it?"

Sarah's voice was shaky as her head popped up from the couch.

"It's me. Ryan," he said. He bent down and picked up the vodka bottle by the couch.

"Huh? What the hell do you want?" Sarah said quietly. The smell of alcohol was strong on her breath.

"I just wanted to check on you."

"Go away." Sarah said as she laid her head back down on the pillow.

"Let me get you some aspirin. Cover your eyes. I'm turning on a light."

"No. No. Just go."

Malone flipped on the light in the kitchen and found a bottle of aspirin in a cabinet. Sarah shaded her eyes with her hand.

"You got any clean cups?"

She didn't answer.

Malone found a cup by the sink that looked relatively clean and filled it with tap water. "Here you go." He held out the cup of water.

"Did you hear me? Go away!" Sarah slapped the cup out of Malone's hand.

He picked it up and shook his head in disgust. "What the hell is going on with you?"

Sarah didn't reply.

Malone went back into the kitchen and saw the stack of unopened mail on the kitchen table. A scowl formed on Malone's face as he stood and looked down at the pile of envelopes. The one on the top was marked past due. He then went back into the living room and heard Sarah crying.

"I'm—uh—a fucking mess," Sarah blurted out. "I know I should cut back on the drinking, but it's the only thing that helps." Tears streaked down Sarah's cheeks.

Malone gently put his hand on Sarah's shoulder.

"I get it. You try talking to someone? A therapist might help. Shit, I've even been talking to someone."

Sarah laughed. "You? Bullshit."

"Yeah. I've been sober for about six weeks."

"You're shitting me."

"No. Really. Not a drop. Look—you've always been a helluva lot smarter than me. You'll figure this out. I know it."

"Thanks. I—hope you're right."

"I got some money for you. I want to help out with some of your bills," Malone held out a roll of cash.

Sarah shook her head no and said, "No. No, don't worry about me."

"It's not a problem, really."

"No. I don't want it," Sarah said as she wiped the tears from her eyes.

"Jesus, you're as stubborn as me, if not worse," Malone mumbled as he stuffed the money in the pocket inside his jacket.

"Go. Just go."

Malone stood there for a moment. "I'll tell you what, I'll go as long as you eat something. Deal?"

Sarah shook her head in disgust. "You're a pain in the ass, you know that?"

"I do indeed," Malone held out the white bag.

Sarah slowly took the bag from him.

"Please let me help. Glad to pay for you to get some help too. Just think about it, okay?"

"Yeah," she said as she nodded her head slowly in agreement.

"Okay," Malone said. He felt his phone vibrate in his pocket and glanced down at it. The call was from Mitchell. He looked back up at Sarah. "I'm serious. If you need anything—not just money—let me know. Really."

Sarah nodded her head in silence as she watched Malone step out the front door.

CHAPTER TEN

"Where the hell are you?" Mitchell said through the phone.

"Just heading back from lunch," Malone said as he climbed into his car. He put the roll of cash into the glove box and covered it with some papers.

"Get your ass back to headquarters. I wanna talk to you," Mitchell said.

"Okay." He realized that he was talking to himself now and hung up. Malone hurried back to headquarters. He had no idea what was bothering her. Malone knocked on the door to Mitchell's office and found her sitting at her desk. She waved him in.

"Sit *down*," she said.

Malone took a seat in the black chair across from her desk.

Mitchell stood by her desk and put her hands on her hips. "I just watched the video footage. This was a surveillance op, and you went and turned it into a goddamn shootout. I've got two team members down now because of you. You're not turning my unit into a fucking shit show."

"They fired on us first. That footage is bullshit. Ask

anyone on the team. I didn't do a damn thing wrong. I followed Ramirez to the Marriott at his request after Cook County SVU was a no-show. We did surveillance on some prostitutes. The Latin Kings were there, and *they* opened fire on us. We took down a few and a few got away. That's it. That's what happened."

"And what about you firing your weapon at a goddamn fire extinguisher in a hotel filled with civilians?"

"It was that or putting even more lives in danger. We had to get out of there. I pulled the fire alarm too."

"You always were a shitty liar."

"Well, then you'd know I ain't lying. It's the truth," Malone said loudly.

Mitchell stared back at Malone, causing him to look away. "Fine. Say I actually believe you. Tell me why the hell I shouldn't bench you? Cook County SVU has twelve people who are assisting us in this op based on the intel we relay to them. This kind of attention is gonna get our asses on the news and you know damn well that Internal Affairs could easily stick their noses in this too."

"This is a helluva lot bigger than you think. EMS found five dead prostitutes that overdosed. I saw some heroin there that I believe was laced with fentanyl. This is a drug problem. Why don't you bring in Narcotics on this?"

Mitchell shifted her hands to her hips. "I don't remember asking your opinion. You're working a prostitution case. The Gang Task Force unit is dead. Get that through your thick skull and get your ass back to work."

"Understood," Malone said carefully. He had to bite his lip. Her words stung like acid. Malone started toward the door.

"One more thing. I'm sending you back to Isley."

"When?" Malone said.

"As soon as possible. You want to be on my squad, you're talking to her at least once a week."

"What the fuck?" Malone mumbled under his breath.

"My unit, my rules." Mitchell crossed her arms.

"Okay. Okay. Fine. I'll do that." His upper lip trembled as he spoke. He turned and left Mitchell's office. It was 1:30 now.

Maybe he could quickly swing by the storage unit before picking up James. He hurried down the hall and went outside. Malone wished he had more time to drop off the cash at the storage unit. He started his car and turned left onto 79th St and followed it to the Dan Ryan Expressway. He flipped on the siren and pressed down on the gas pedal, cutting past the other vehicles. Malone glanced over to his left and saw an L train slowing as it stopped at the 35th Street station.

Malone turned off the siren and then checked his rearview mirror. He saw a black Chevy Tahoe that looked like an unmarked police vehicle. He sped up again and continued to cut through traffic, moving past a few other cars. When he flicked his eyes up, the black Tahoe was still a few cars back. Malone pulled his foot off of the gas and a few other vehicles passed him. The Tahoe was still there, not any closer to Malone. Malone's stomach sank. He tried to ignore the feeling. He knew he was being followed.

Malone continued to slow down. The black Tahoe got closer. Malone suddenly swerved over two lanes to the right, cutting off a gray Chevy Silverado and then a white semi. Horns honked and brakes squealed. Malone looked to the left to see the profile of a blonde woman in the black Tahoe. It looked a lot like Teresa Warner of Internal Affairs, but he wasn't totally sure. He rubbed his eyes and pulled off at the 31st Street exit.

His mind raced a million miles a minute, bouncing from one thought to another. Warner. Ann. James. Redford. A drink. Max. Mitchell. Ann. A drink. The cash. Johnny. Junior. The shootout in the hotel. A drink. Ramirez. Mitchell. James. A drink. The cash.

The harsh chemical smell of the fire extinguisher was still in his nose and made it harder to think clearly. He thought of stopping to get some coffee, but knew that caffeine was the last thing he really needed. It would only make him more anxious. Suddenly, he felt the air squeeze out of his lungs. Malone clenched his chest and struggled to breathe. His heart pounded heavily, and he heard the blood pumping in his ears.

He jerked the wheel, causing the car to pullover to the side of the road. He was convinced that this time it was really a heart attack, but his arms weren't tingling. He was still conscious. It was just more palpitations. The pounding worsened. Thump. Thump. Each heartbeat grew louder in his head. Thump. Thump. He thought about dialing 911, but knew they wouldn't likely do a damn thing other than take him to the hospital for observation.

Malone needed a distraction. He needed help. He picked up his phone.

"Hello?"

"Hey, it's Ryan," Malone said.

"Ryan Malone. You got a nasty habit of only calling me when you need something. Tell me this ain't one of those times," Morgan said in a groggy voice.

"Well—uh—it's nice to be needed, ain't it?"

"Fuck you, you Irish bastard," Morgan snapped.

"Guilty as charged," Malone laughed. "I just wanted to talk to you for a minute. Could really use your help."

"Oh? What about? You never talk very much," Morgan said.

"I'm having heart palpitations. Scaring the shit out of me.

Goes away after a bit, but I thought you might be able to help."

"Sorry to hear that," Morgan said. "Uh—you know—it usually means you're overdoing it. Stress and anxiety just pile up over time and it only gets worse. Press pause. Step back. Try to figure out what is causing you a lot of worry."

"Well, you know I quit drinking after that close call a little while ago."

"Close call my ass. You had one foot in the grave. Ain't that about right?"

"I guess—"

"You on any medication?"

"I was on some oxy for a while after being shot."

"When'd you stop taking it?"

"Couple days ago."

"Any other symptoms?"

"Rapid heartbeat. Nausea. Feeling pretty achy. Like I'm kinda hungover."

"Damn. You could be in opiate withdrawal. You quit cold turkey?"

"Shit—uh. Kinda. What should I do?"

"Close your eyes. Take a deep breath and exhale. Try and breathe as deeply as you can. I'm serious. Do it."

Morgan paused and silence filled the air.

"Okay. Are you doing that?" Morgan said.

"Yeah. Yeah, I am." Malone replied.

"Now think about whatever makes you feel good. I don't care if it's putting handcuffs on a perp or some bimbo with big tits. Whatever takes you to your happy place. Get away from all the shit. Go there. Focus your attention on something good."

"My happy place, huh?" Malone tried to stifle his laughter.

"Yep. Not dating assholes is what takes me to my happy

place. I'll take a good book, a hot bath, and a glass of wine instead."

"Okay. I got it." Malone closed his eyes and took another deep breath. "I think this is really helping."

"Good. You really should finish your prescription too and take a couple days off work. You gotta taper down with the opiates. You can't go cold turkey with that shit."

"Okay. Thanks for talking with me."

"You're welcome. Now how about you call me sometime when you don't need something?"

"Deal." Malone hung up and continued deep breathing. After a few minutes, the heart palpitations were manageable. They were still there in the background, but not as loud. Malone decided to go home and to get his prescription. Morgan was probably right. Going cold turkey was stupid.

He drove to his apartment and hurried inside. He grumbled as he reached into the trashcan, pulled the pills out, and wiped off the coffee grounds with a paper towel. Quickly, he took two pills and put the rest into a pill bottle and slipped it into his jacket pocket. He took the white paper bag that had held the donuts and pulled out a powder one and ate it in just a few quick bites. He then washed it down with a glass of water. Having something in his stomach made him feel a little better.

Malone left his apartment and got back into his car. He took a few deep breaths and then carefully pulled out onto the road. His phone rang. An unknown phone number with an odd area code.

"Hello?" Malone said.

"Hello, is this Sergeant Ryan Malone?"

"Yeah, that's me. Who's this?"

"You came into my shop over a month ago about a U-Haul truck. I'm Martin Brickman."

"Who?"

"Martin Brickman. I have a used car lot and go by Marty.

"Oh yeah, Marty. What's going on?"

"I—uh—have two cargo vans that I rented out and they're on their way to Chicago. I have GPS on all of my vehicles now."

"Why does this matter to me?" Malone said.

"I want to be sure to get the vans back. The drivers acted suspicious and had guns. They were coming from California and arrived in moving truck, then split the load between two vans."

"Tell me about these guns," Malone replied.

"They were large guns, looked like they were military or something."

"Okay. Do you the names for these drivers?"

"Juan Gutierrez and Albert Rivera."

"What's the current location on these vans?"

"Yeah. Both are about an hour from Chicago, traveling together. Just a few miles from the Illinois border."

"Okay, good. Call me when the vans are a half hour out from Chicago."

"Will do."

Malone thought about calling the DEA, but decided to not do it. Bureaucracies moved like a snail so they couldn't do anything in an hour.

He then remembered James and Ann. *Shit*. He called Tricia, Ann's mother. The call rang and rang. Finally, it went to voicemail. "Hey Tricia, it's Ryan. Can you do me a big favor and pickup James at school? Been having car problems. Just let me know. Thanks."

Malone then called Carver.

"I got something urgent for the team to look into."

"Huh? What's the rush?"

"Got a tip on a new shipment coming from San Diego into Chicago. Coming in soon."

"Soon? How soon?"

"In the next half hour or so," Malone said.

"Look, Malone—I got the team in the field and they're deep in something else right now."

"This is reliable. Could even lead to some bigger fish."

"I hear you, but I'm afraid I ain't got the manpower to look into it. Sorry."

"Yeah. Yeah. All right." Malone hung up. He looked at the time. 2:15. He tried calling Tricia again. Nothing. The call went to voicemail. Malone scowled as he slapped the steering wheel with his hands. He tried calling Ann.

"Hey, are you on your way to pick up James?"

"Hey, well, I'm actually having car trouble. Got a flat tire too. I don't think I'm gonna make it over there on time. Can you call the school and figure something out?"

"Yeah, I guess—"

"Thanks," Malone said quickly and hung up.

Malone drove north of Chicago on the Kennedy Expressway, just past Wicker Park. It was a bit of a gamble taking I-90, but it was the route that made the most sense. More cars meant more cover, so a shipment would be less likely to be discovered. He heard his phone ring and picked it up.

"Yeah?"

"It looks like both vans are heading south and sticking together," Marty said.

"Okay. I'm waiting by exit 50B East Ohio Street," Malone said. "Can you see how far that is on your GPS?"

"Yeah, just a couple minutes out from there," Marty said.

Malone could feel the sweat forming on his brow as he watched his rearview mirror for two white rental vans. He thought he saw something off in the distance, but a semi switched lanes blocking visibility. Malone moved to the far left lane and saw the two white vans approaching. He got back over to the center lane and waited. He had to stay back and not get too close.

He followed the two vans down I-90 to the South Wentworth exit. Then the vans turned down Root Street and then merged left onto Exchange Avenue. From a distance, Malone saw the vans turn right into an alleyway behind a faded brick warehouse with a white for lease sign on the side of it. Malone went past the alleyway and drove around the block and found some open parking on the street. He knew he couldn't see shit unless he got closer.

He found an open alleyway and hurried down it with his P226 in hand. The back of the alleyway led to an empty parking lot. To the left was another lot full of construction rentals. Forklifts and towable generators, flatbeds and backhoes, excavators and more. Malone took the roll of cash from his jacket and put it in the glovebox, covering it up with some napkins. Then he hurried across the railroad tracks and used some trees behind a row of semi trailers for cover. On the other side of the trailers, he spotted the two vans. Malone crouched down and made his way toward them. Two young Latino men were unloading crates and one older Latino man stood there watching. A couple other black men dressed in black jackets came out from the warehouse.

Malone tightened his grip on his P226 and wanted to engage the enemy, but he knew five on one was nothing short of a suicide mission. Malone recognized one of the men as Darius Jones, an up-and-comer for the Gangster Disciples. Darius handed over a bag to one of the Latino men.

He opened it and looked at the contents.

"Where's the rest?" the man said loudly.

"Rest? What you mean rest?"

"This ain't right. What the hell you doin' shorting us?"

"The fuck it ain't. We ain't rippin you off," Darius said. "We agreed on fifty."

"No, it ain't. It's seventy-five," the Latino said.

"Shit. What? Says who?"

The Latino man looked over at one of the other drivers who nodded in agreement.

"You owe twenty-five more," the Latino man said.

"Twenty-five more? Shit. A'ight. A'ight. Lemme get the money." Darius came back with another bag. He pulled a shotgun out of the bag and fired, shooting one of the drivers in the chest. The other Latino driver drew a 9mm and fired back, but missed wide. Darius then shot him in the chest with another shotgun blast. The last one, the older man, put his hands in the air. The other Gangster Disciple, a younger teen named Lil' Joe, fired a 9mm and killed the last man. The old man was still breathing. Darius fired another blast at the man on the ground.

Malone froze. He couldn't think, he couldn't act. His hands started shaking. He braced himself as he put his finger on the trigger. Something stopped him from engaging. Malone stayed in position, watching the men.

The men took the dead bodies into the back of the vans and then drove the vans into the warehouse.

Malone slowly approached the warehouse. He carefully tested the doorknob. It was unlocked. He stood with his back up against the building listening. He couldn't hear anything, so he carefully turned and slipped inside the door. Inside were rows and rows of countless crates, barrels, and boxes. This definitely wasn't a lab.

There was an office to the right and several other closed doors. Malone glanced under them to see that no lights were on. Malone quickly moved past the doors and approached the many shipping containers, crates, boxes, and barrels. He thought he heard some men talking and immediately hid behind some crates. Once he knew it was clear, he crept through the warehouse using the boxes for cover.

The voices grew louder. Soon, three men were standing there. Two from outside and one man with his back turned to Malone.

A young voice said, "Hey, boss."

The man turned around.

Malone's gut sank. It was Ace. It took everything in Malone to not fire his gun immediately. This bastard killed two cops and deserved to die.

"Five-oh gonna be coming by after all that damn noise out there. What the hell you thinkin?" Ace said.

"Hadta do it," Darius said.

"That right?" Ace replied.

"Yep. Fuckers was trying to rip us off. I'm telling ya—" Lil' Joe said.

"Look, just fucking get to it," Ace interrupted. "Why you put 'em in the vans? Toss'em in some barrels fore I toss your ass in one too."

The men nodded and took the bodies out of the back of the van. Then they pushed one of the bodies into an empty blue barrel and then closed it up.

Malone weighed his options. He didn't want to let Ace get away, but he couldn't do this on his own. He snuck back out the entrance and called for backup. "10-1, 10-1 shots fired Halstead and Exchange. Crime in progress, lights only, no sirens. Repeat no sirens. Requesting SWAT assistance. Over?"

"10-4. No sirens. Requesting SWAT. All available officers please assist."

Malone waited in the quiet parking lot. He couldn't help but wonder if he made the right call. He wanted to kill Ace and never spend another moment worrying about him ever again. That would be a small taste of justice. But as he waited alone, justice felt far out away.

In a matter of minutes, the warehouse was surrounded by police. CPD officers were in position both to the left and right of Malone. SWAT rolled up in an Army brown Lenco Bearcat armored vehicle.

Malone stayed in position watching the warehouse and one of the SWAT officers came up next to him.

"What the hell is going on?" A SWAT team member in a green uniform said to Malone.

Malone recognized the voice. "Hey, Carter. How are ya?"

"Not bad. Been on SWAT for about a month," Carter said.

"Good for you. Can't get away from wearing that Army green, can you?"

"Guess not. What do we got here?"

"Got at least three armed Gangster Disciples inside. They already killed three people who appeared to be drug runners. They took the bodies inside the warehouse. A shit ton of crates and barrels in there, likely drugs. I suspect some contain heroin or fentanyl precursor."

"You went inside?" Carter said.

"Just a peek. About ten minutes ago."

"Any civilians?"

"Unknown. Didn't see any, though." Malone kept his eyes focused on the doorway to the warehouse.

"All right." Carter stood up and started to walk back to the large vehicle.

"Hey, Carter."

Carter turned around. "Yeah?"

"Ugly prick with burn marks on his neck is Ace. He's a goddamn cop killer."

Carter nodded once and went back to the rest of the SWAT team who were standing by the back of the vehicle. The SWAT team included seven men: Jake Carter, Jack Morris, Brandon White, Brett Simmons, Drew Harris, Shane Hagen, and Vince Fisher.

Morris ordered two uniformed officers, Matt Davis and

Lauren Tracey, to the other side of the warehouse and instructed them to watch the other door to the building on Halstead.

Once Davis called to confirm they were in position, SWAT approached the building in standard formation with gas masks on, AR-15 rifles, and shields. SWAT carefully entered through the door.

Once inside, Morris sent part of the team to the office. Carter took the first door and Harris backed him up. It was a break room with some vending machines, a coffee machine, and tables. Nothing. Harris took the second room and Morris backed him up. This room was an empty maintenance closet with some supplies and a mop and tools. Simmons and Fisher took the next room, a bathroom with just one small toilet and sink. Carter took the last room. It was just another small office, so small that it wasn't much more than a desk with a window and a closet. Nothing. Morris met the men by the main door.

On the other side of the warehouse, a loud crash. Someone cursed loudly. Morris led the team toward the noise and saw one of the blue barrels had fallen over with a pair of feet sticking out the top of it. A man was standing next to the barrel, trying to tip it upright. Blood was on the ground.

"Shit! These damn plastic barrels is slick," Lil' Joe said.

Another man walked up and laughed. "No man, you just weak." The man turned around and revealed the scars on his neck. It was Ace.

"Fuck you," the young man said to Ace.

Ace just glared back. "Yo. You gonna give 'em a hand?" Ace said to Darius.

"Yeah, yeah." Darius walked over.

Both men bent over and carefully tipped up the barrel.

"What we doing with his feet, man?" Lil' Joe asked.

"Chainsaw, man," Ace replied.

"What? You jokin' right?"

Ace smiled and said, "That or a regular saw."

"Huh? What?" Lil' Joe replied with wide eyes.

Ace shrugged. "Just push 'em in the barrel and seal it. You can bend 'em. He ain't gonna feel nothin." Ace got a message and glanced at his phone.

As the team approached, the popping sound of a 9mm came out of nowhere. Carter saw who was firing and quickly returned fire. Lil' Joe fell to the ground.

Ace noticed a small stream of fentanyl precursor trickled from the blue barrel down onto the concrete floor. He quickly fired two blasts from his shotgun, causing more liquid to splash down onto the floor. He turned and ran toward the other side of the building. Darius picked up Lil' Joe off of the ground and the two men followed.

"Stop! We gotta get the fuck out!" Morris barked out through his gas mask. All seven men hurried back out of the warehouse. Ace went out the side entrance that led down a small alley and turned right, heading to the road.

"Freeze! Chicago PD!" Tracey said with her Glock pointed at Ace's head.

He froze, dropped his weapon, and put his hands up. Lil' Joe dropped his gun and Darius fired his shotgun. The blast hit Tracey, slamming into her chest and knocking her down.

Ace picked up his gun and saw Davis coming down the alley. He fired a couple rounds and Davis ducked for cover. Ace, Darius, and Lil' Joe cut across the alley to the street. Ace saw a silver Toyota Corolla coming down the street and ran towards it with the shotgun drawn. The car stopped and the driver jumped out. All three men climbed into the car and sped down Halstead.

Malone ran to the door when SWAT come back out.

"What the *fuck* happened?" Malone screamed.

Carter pulled off his gas mask. "Got a massive chemical leak in there. One of the blue barrels is spraying shit all over."

"Tracey, Davis, do you read me? Tracey, Davis, you there?" Harris said into his radio.

No response at all.

"Shit! What the hell happened?" Malone barked out to no one in particular. He ran around to the other side of the warehouse. Carter and Harris followed close behind.

"Officer down! I—can't get a pulse! I need an ambo now!" a voice said over the radio. Malone realized it was Davis.

Once they got to the other side of the building, they found Davis on his knees checking Tracey's vitals. Blood was all over his hands.

Davis stayed on the ground and moved on to doing chest compressions on Tracey. "I ain't fucking getting nothing," Davis snarled in frustration.

"Let me take over." Malone kneeled on the ground and continued doing chest compressions.

"I don't know what the fuck happened. Assholes came out blasting. Then they disappeared." Davis said. "They disappeared and now she's fucking gone!"

"I'm not giving up," Malone said as he continued chest compressions.

Carter looked down at Tracey's body. "Malone," Carter said in a normal voice.

Tracey didn't respond to the chest compressions.

"Malone," Carter said louder.

Malone pressed harder on Tracey and sweat formed on his forehead.

"Malone!" Carter barked.

Malone looked over at Carter.

"It's time to stop. Really."

Malone's mouth hung open as he looked at the ground where Tracey laid in front of him. He felt her blood on his fingertips and noticed his hands were shaking.

"This bullshit's gotta stop," Malone growled. "What the fuck are we doing? Cause this shit sure ain't working."

Malone sat on the ground feeling numb and his hands continued shaking. He wanted to scream, he wanted to cry, he wanted to grab Ace around the neck and never let go. Davis asked Malone to help him file a report and he told him to fuck off. He got up and walked to his car that he'd parked over on Exchange Avenue.

His thoughts were racing. As he drove toward the Save A Lot parking lot near West 80th Street, he saw the liquor store across the street to the right. Traffic stopped and he waited for the light to change ahead. He closed his eyes and took another deep breath. He didn't open his eyes until someone behind him honked the horn. The light was now green.

As he turned onto West 32nd, he saw Gino's Tavern on the left side of the road. He pulled his foot off the gas pedal when he saw an empty parking space on the street. Suddenly, a black truck swerved toward Malone's car and sideswiped it. Malone jerked the wheel and lost control. The sound of metal crashing into metal was followed by the shattering of glass. His head slammed face first into a white airbag that covered the steering wheel. His face was numb.

Something wet and sticky streamed down from his nose. From the metallic taste, he knew it was blood. He thought he heard what sounded like people screaming or voices crying out.

Everything turned black.

CHAPTER ELEVEN

Malone opened his eyes and felt something sticky on his face. The airbag had exploded, and the chemicals smelled like a combination of smoke and gunpowder. He slowly got out of the car and lost his balance, tumbling onto the ground. He saw that he crashed into a navy blue Taurus parked on the side of the road. He sat up with his back against the side of his car and caught his breath.

In the distance, he heard sirens. He must have been out for a couple minutes. His nose was bleeding and he wiped off the blood with his face with the back of his hand. The pain would start soon.

The sirens got louder and Malone knew the ambulance would arrive soon. Malone's grit his teeth and his lip started to quiver. He had a job to do, and nothing was going to stop him. The ambulance pulled up and two male EMTs quickly pulled a stretcher from the back.

"I'm fine, I'm fine. Go the fuck away," Malone snapped. He pulled himself up off the ground and leaned against the side of the car. Malone saw the two EMTs approaching out of the corner of his eye.

"No, no. I'm fine." Malone shooed them back with his hand.

"Sir, are you okay? You were in a car accident. We need to take you to the hospital." One of the EMTs got closer.

"No. I'm fine. Did you fucking hear me?" Malone barked.

"Sir, you need medical attention," an EMT said.

"Just lemme catch my goddamn breath."

"Sit here. Let us check your vitals," one of the EMTs said.

"Fine," Malone sat down on the stretcher with his legs hanging over.

The first EMT took Malone's pulse and the other EMT watched him breathe. Then the first EMT then checked Malone's eyes with a flashlight. "Follow the light with your eyes."

Malone followed along.

"Sir, your eyes aren't tracking well, and that's often a sign of concussion. Can you see all right?"

"Yeah. I can see fine. Really," Malone said with a shrug.

"Let us take you to the ER just to get checked out."

"No. I ain't going to the hospital for a goddamn fender bender."

"Sir, did you see what happened to your vehicle?"

Malone looked over at his black Chevy. Most of the front end was smashed in. The front windshield was broken and cracked. The driver's side front quarter panel was smashed in too.

"Yeah, I was the one driving." Malone said.

"Come on, sir, let us take you to the ER."

"I told you, I'm fine."

"Okay," EMT said with a sigh as he started moving the stretcher back to the ambulance.

A police cruiser rolled up with the sirens blaring.

"Shit," Malone mumbled to himself. He remembered that he left that cash inside the car. Malone reached back into the car and the airbag had deployed on the passenger side. He reached under the deployed airbag and tried to open the glove box. It didn't want to budge.

An officer came to the car door. "Hello, are you okay?" she asked.

Malone recognized her from the 9th precinct. Her name was Angie Hall.

"Yeah," Malone said. "I'm okay." Malone continued to pull at the glove box.

"Forget something?" Hall said.

"Yeah. Not gonna leave my cigars here," Malone said with his back to the officer. He finally got the glove compartment to open and slipped the cash into his inner jacket pocket. Then he slowly got out of the car. He pulled out a cigar from his coat and stuck it between his teeth. "Got a light?"

"Afraid not," Hall said.

"It's all right," Malone said with a slight smile.

"What happened?"

"Someone sideswiped me, and I hit the back of that car.

"Shit. You okay?"

"Yeah. But if you got any aspirin, I won't turn 'em down," Malone said.

Hall walked over to look at the front of Malone's car and then the other car that he hit. "You're lucky you just got a few bumps and bruises after this mess." Hall said.

"Yeah, you're right." Malone replied.

"I'll call the tow truck. Safe to say your car is totaled. I'll have to get your official statement."

"Sure, if you promise to make it quick."

"Trust me, I don't like paperwork anymore than you do," Hall said with a smile.

Something about Hall reminded him of Ann. Maybe it was her hair color, maybe it was her voice, or her personality. Maybe it was all of the above.

Hall walked back to her cruiser to get the paperwork.

Malone leaned against the rear of his car, found his lighter in his jacket and lit his cigar. He tried to calm himself, but he couldn't. He could only think of catching Ace.

Malone and Hall filled out the paperwork together. Malone found it hard to concentrate, and he had to let Hall write up the report. As they sat in the cruiser, a tow truck pulled up. Malone watched as the driver pulled the Chevy onto the tow truck.

"You kinda look like you're saying goodbye to an old friend or something," Hall said.

"Huh? What's that?" Malone asked quietly as he watched the tow truck drive off.

"Nothing," Hall said with a smile. "I think that's it for the paperwork. Can I give you a lift?"

"Yeah, that'd be great. I'm just going back to headquarters."

"You sure?" Hall looked over at Malone with wide eyes as she looked at the dried blood on his face.

"Yeah, I'm fine. I'll just get cleaned up there."

"Okay," Hall said as she drove the police cruiser down the road.

CHAPTER TWELVE

Malone walked into police headquarters and went directly to the locker room. He cleaned himself up at the sink and changed into a fresh t-shirt. He didn't have a change of pants, but his jeans were dark and didn't look too bad. Walking toward the Vice office, he noticed that his balance was a bit off. Or maybe his legs were just weak. He stopped walking and leaned against the wall.

"Hey. You all right?" Carver asked, a stack of files in one hand and a cup of coffee in the other.

"No. I'm not okay. I'm really fucking far from okay."

"I get it. I heard what happened. Tracey was good police. I'm sorry I couldn't help out earlier." Malone followed Carver into his office.

"Yeah. I know. It's alright. Nothing you could do."

Carver turned around and put his hand on Malone's shoulder. "You did the right thing calling in SWAT."

"If you say so. Helluva job they did."

"I get it. Look, if you want to be transferred over to Narcotics, I might be able to get it to go through, especially after this thing at the warehouse. You're great with tracking down drugs, and we could really use you here."

"Sounds good to me."

"Okay. I'll see what I can do."

Malone nodded in agreement. "Since you're in the mood for favors, you got any pull in motor pool? I need a vehicle. I got in a fender bender, and my car was totaled."

"Shit. You okay?"

"Yeah. I'll survive. Just a little shaken up. A few bumps and bruises, that's all."

"Let me guess. You refused to go to the ER, right?"

"I don't need some stupid quack telling me I'm fine."

"Why don't you just take mine, eh? Just don't light up any of those cheap ass cigars in it."

Carver tossed Malone the keys.

"You know, I think you gave me some of those cigars," Malone shot back.

Carver laughed. "You're full of shit, Malone."

Malone smiled.

"Seriously, don't smoke in it."

"Thanks. Where'd you park?"

"Second level of the deck. By the stairs."

"Anything new on Ace or those other pricks?"

"Not that I've heard. An APB out on him and the other two. We'll get 'em. Be more careful, will ya?"

Malone nodded in agreement and hurried out of the station. After he climbed the stairs in the parking deck, he pressed the key fob and heard a beep come from a white Crown Victoria with a blue stripe and red lettering.

"Shit," Malone said as he climbed inside. It was better than nothing, but he wouldn't be sneaking up on anyone anytime soon.

Malone got back into the cruiser and cruised around for an hour just looking for any familiar faces on familiar corners.

No one was out, the streets were quiet. As he was driving around, he saw Windy City Pawn and decided to stop. He parked on the street across from the store.

"Man, what you doin' driving that thing?" Erv said in a serious tone as Malone walked inside.

Malone chuckled. "My car got totaled. Better than walkin', you know?"

"People gonna think I got held up again."

"I'll make it quick."

"Make it fast and in a hurry too," Erv said.

"Fine. You got any line on where Ace or any other Gangster Disciples are setting up shop?"

Erv shook his head no. "Nope. 'Fraid not. They gettin' better at movin' all around."

"Yeah, I bet. I was wondering, you ever get any guns in here?"

"You kidding me? You know I can't buy, sell, or pawn firearms in Cook County."

"Just looking for something for my wife." Malone shrugged.

Erv held his hand up to his chin and stroked his beard. "Your wife, huh? Gimme a second." Erv disappeared into the back of the store. Malone drummed his fingers on the counter as he waited. A moment later, Erv had a nickel finish S&W Model 10 revolver in his hand and held it out flat in front of Malone.

Malone picked up the gun and held it in his hand. The number had been filed off. It had good balance. He opened the cylinder. It was empty.

"Think that'll work?"

Malone nodded in agreement. "Got any ammo?"

"Here," Erv said as he set a half-full box of ammo on the counter.

"I appreciate you taking care of me earlier. This one on

the house. Keep your girl safe," Erv said. "But you didn't get any of that from me."

Malone smiled and nodded. "Where'd you get it?" Malone asked as he checked the sights on the gun.

"Really wanna know?" Erv asked.

"Just tell me."

Erv exhaled and clicked his tongue. "Think this one was from a dancer. She had it for protection. Got it from her boyfriend who was a Latin King. I ain't saying this gun is clean. It probably ain't. Anyhow, she ain't dancing no more."

"Shit," Malone said, "just thought of something. Thanks, man." Malone grabbed the box of ammo and tucked the gun into his belt as he hurried out the exit.

He tore down the street. The car fishtailed as he turned right onto Archer Avenue. The hairs on his neck stood up as he made a quick left on to S. Canal Street. He exhaled as he approached the tall brick building with the black canopy marked The Pink Monkey in bright pink letters. He hadn't been there since he told a dancer, Vi, that Max had died. Revisiting a location filled with bad memories wasn't a great idea, but he had no other choice. He wanted Ace, and this was one of the best places to find him.

He parked to the side of the building in the public parking lot with a short black metal fence around it. Next to the public parking was the lot for the employees. He immediately recognized a yellow car in the lot and looked away.

The club was busier than he expected it to be in the afternoon. A blonde dancer in a pink thong danced to some AC/DC on a small stage covered in pink lights. The customers—all men—sat in light brown leather chairs at small square tables as they watched the dancer on stage. Malone walked to the bar and waited for a brunette bartender in a black leather bikini to notice him.

"Whaddya want?" The bartender continued to pour a mixed drink and didn't look up.

"Vi here?" Malone said.

"I dunno," the bartender snapped.

"Can you check? I'd like to talk to her. Please. I'm a friend."

The bartender glared back at Malone and disappeared. As Malone waited, he turned around to avoid facing the liquor bottles lined up behind the bar. He sat down on a stool and glanced around the club. Another dancer appeared on stage, and someone turned up the volume for the Def Leppard song that blared over the sound system. No familiar faces were sitting at any of the tables or at the bar. But it was pretty hard to tell who was there with the pink lights covering the entire room. The music finally stopped, and the dancer left the stage.

Someone tapped his shoulder. It was Vi. She had a big pink boa around her neck and bright red lipstick. Same curly black hair. Seeing her again was a knife twisting in the gut. Vi's eyes widened when she realized it was Malone. "Can we talk in private?" Malone said, not wanting to compete with the loud guitar chords of the next song.

Vi nodded and Malone followed her to the VIP section. A big bouncer was waiting there behind the velvet red rope and didn't say a word.

He followed Vi down the hallway and sat down in the chair in the middle of the small room. She stood in front of Malone and started to dance.

"You don't have to do that," Malone said.

"A lot less questions if I dance," Vi said.

"Okay, whatever you want. I was hoping you could help me find someone. I'll make it worth your while."

"Who?"

"Gangster Disciple that goes by Ace. Ugly motherfucker

that used to have a big cursive A on his neck. Now there's a big scar there."

"Why you want him?" Vi turned around and shook her ass at Malone.

"I—uh—he's a cop killer and distributing drugs," Malone said. "A real piece of shit."

"Can't say I've seen anyone matching that description lately," Vi said, looking Malone right in the eye.

"You see any other Gangster Disciples here?"

"Always a few popping up. But not that one."

Vi turned around and straddled Malone's lap and moved up and down.

"Call me if you see him?" Malone said.

"Yeah, I will. Sure."

"Good. Thanks."

Vi stood up.

"You need my number?" Malone said.

"No, I know how to get ahold of you."

"Okay. Good. Thanks for your help."

"You got it," Vi said.

Seeing Vi reopened some fresh wounds. Malone went to the bathroom and splashed some water on his face. He popped a few aspirin, then went back to the bar and paid way too much for a club soda with lime and half-watched the dancer on stage. He waited through a couple songs and then made his way out to the parking lot.

Malone got back to the police cruiser. He called Ann who picked up on the second ring.

"Hey," Ann said. "What the hell happened? I called a bunch of times and you never answered. Every call went straight to voicemail. What the hell is going on?"

"Sorry about that. I've been out in the field all day. I'll tell you more when I get home."

"That mean you're on your way now?"

"Yeah," Malone said with a yawn. "I'm in my car. I'll be there pretty quick."

"Okay. Good. Please hurry. We need to talk."

"Yeah. Sounds good." Malone scowled as he hung up. He didn't want to go home. What he really wanted was to get Ace. And he wanted him worse than ever before.

CHAPTER THIRTEEN

Malone slowed the police car to a stop in front of the house and stayed inside. After sitting there for a while, he didn't know what to say other than he was sorry. He knew he couldn't tell Ann exactly what happened. He would have to just make up a story on the fly. When he got to the door, he wasn't sure if he should knock or go right in. He decided to knock just to be safe. After he knocked, time seemed to slow down. It seemed like forever.

Ann slowly opened the door and had a blank expression on her face.

Malone wasn't sure if that was good or bad.

"Where the hell have you been?" Ann said quietly.

"Huh? Just been working."

"And you couldn't get James? My Mom had to pick him up. She said you called in a panic and left a voicemail? I had to take the L home and couldn't get ahold to you."

"It was urgent, I promise. I was on a stakeout."

Ann looked down at the sidewalk and avoided eye contact with Malone.

"Why didn't you call me earlier?" Ann blurted out.

"I got put in the field at the last minute, and I wanted to help you out." Malone could feel the sweat forming on his upper lip as he spoke. He also knew she could snap at any moment.

"You know—"

"I'm sorry. I fucked up," Malone blurted out.

Ann looked up and glared at Malone. "Let me talk! It drives me crazy when you interrupt me."

"Sorry."

"What the hell am I supposed to think? Do you think I don't watch the news? I know about the police officer getting killed today," Ann said loudly. "You were there weren't you? You could have been dead too."

Malone didn't respond.

"Tell me, are we always going to be a distant second to your job? You say you love me, and then you pull this kind of shit? What about your son? You never spend time with him. He barely *knows* you."

"You're right. You're right. Of course, I want to be with you. I'm clean. I'm sober. I'm a different person now."

Ann crossed her arms. "You may not be drinking, but that doesn't mean you're not an addict. You're addicted to your job. You can't quit. Over the past couple days, you've been working nonstop."

"Mmm-hmm," Malone shifted his eyes away from Ann's for a moment. "Yeah. You're right."

"Look at me," Ann said firmly.

Malone's eyes darted back to Ann's.

"I'm done. I can't do this anymore. You gotta choose. Us or the job. Quit trying to pretend you can do both. It's bull-shit, and you know it. Keep doing what you're doing, and it's a countdown until you leave again. Or I get the call that you're in the morgue."

"No—no. I'm not. I'm here. I'm never gonna make that mistake again. I'm here."

"I know you, Ryan. I know how you're wired. Maybe not for a few months or a maybe even a year, but it's just a matter of time until you're gone."

"Look, I'm not leaving you. I'm the same guy I've always been. The same guy you married. But you can't ask me to be someone else. I love the job. I wanna make a difference."

Tears streamed down Ann's face. She wiped one off of her cheek with her hand. "The worst thing," Ann said, "is you think you love it. That you love being a cop. You really hate it. You're just too damn stubborn to admit it."

"Look—I *choose* you. I *choose* James. *Really*. Give me a few days to wrap up some shit. If I don't, I'm gonna always wonder if I could've done more."

"Fine. You've got a couple more days, then you're done."

Malone stepped forward and embraced Ann. He then followed her inside and sat on the couch.

"I have no clue what I'm gonna to do," Malone said.

"I don't either. But we'll get you. That's enough," Ann said.

Both were quiet for a while until Ann broke the silence.

"You know, you'd make one helluva a Walmart greeter," Ann said with a quiet laugh.

"James'd use that to get more toys," Malone said.

"You're right, he would."

Malone yawned. "Speaking of which, is he in bed?"

"Yeah, he is," Ann replied.

"Okay," Malone said quietly trying to cover up a yawn.

"You should get some rest. I can tell you're running on fumes here," Ann said.

"Yeah, I should," Malone said.

"Go ahead. I may or may not be up later."

He quickly fell asleep on the bed and slept harder than he

had in a really long time. He dreamed and dreamed, but when he woke up, he couldn't remember any of the details from his dreams. He turned to the right later in the night and saw Ann fast asleep. Malone's eyes were heavy and his thoughts were clouded. He felt hungover despite not having had a drop of alcohol. He got up and went to the bathroom, and accidentally bumped the toilet. The toilet seat slammed down, waking Ann.

"Huh?" Ann said as she sat bolt upright in bed.

"Sorry, it's just me. Can't sleep, so I'm getting ready for work," Malone whispered.

Ann looked over at the alarm clock. "It's 5:05, why not sleep a little longer?"

"I gotta wrap some stuff up," Malone said.

"You want coffee?"

"No, no. That's okay. I'll get some at the station. I'm just gonna grab a quick shower and go. I only got a couple days before I'm retired."

"Okay," Ann said as she laid back down.

"Do I—uh—still have some more clothes here?" Malone asked as he rubbed his eyes.

"On top of the dresser."

Malone looked over at the dresser and saw a change of clothes. "Thanks." As he stood in the shower, he waited for his headache to fade. Finally, he started to feel better. He took some aspirin from the medicine cabinet just to be safe and got dressed. When he walked back to the bedroom, Ann was gone. He stepped down the stairs to the living room, and found Ann half asleep on the couch covered in a blue fleece blanket.

"I'm gonna go. I love you," Malone whispered and kissed Ann on the cheek.

"Love you too," Ann said, half asleep.

Malone glanced back in through the window to see Ann

and then drove down the dark street. He knew Ann meant every word she said. This was it. Now or never. The thought of soon being unemployed gave Malone an empty feeling in the pit of his stomach. The only thing he ever knew how to be was a cop. He knew it'd be a lot like losing an arm or a leg. He wouldn't be able to function like he did before.

Malone parked on the first floor of the parking deck next to the station. Before getting out of the car, he closed his eyes. He pictured himself jumping off of a diving board and instead of landing in a pool, he just saw himself falling. As he exhaled, he opened his eyes and felt some small sense of relief knowing he wouldn't have to worry about cash for a time. The cash in the storage unit would be enough to take care of bills for a while, even with large portions of it going to other families. Sure, he'd eventually have to find something else to do, but for at least the next six months or so, they would be fine. More importantly, Ann and James would still be in his life. While it would suck not being a cop, it was better than being divorced and alone.

Nothing would stop him from keeping his promise he made to Ann. He owed her that. Malone didn't really want to walk away from the job, but he really didn't have a choice. He loved her. He loved James. And he couldn't put them through more hell. His thoughts jumbled together in his mind like a puzzle and the pieces kept changing. The only problem he could think about now was getting Ace. No more excuses. He would find him and get him. The clock was ticking now, and there was no going back.

CHAPTER FOURTEEN

With each passing moment, Malone only got more anxious and impatient. He heard his phone ring and pulled it out of his jacket pocket. One missed call from an unknown Chicago area number. The caller didn't leave a voicemail. He wondered who it was from, but had other things to handle right now.

When Malone got to headquarters, he went directly to Vice and sat down at his desk. He started working on his resignation letter. As he typed the first sentence, he paused and pinched the bridge of his nose. His fingers pecked on the keys and two more sentences appeared on the screen. He sighed as he read the words. Malone wanted to write something more, but the words wouldn't come. It was only three sentences long. Nothing fancy at all. Malone printed out the document and held the piece of paper in his hands. He glanced it over and scratched his signature on the page in blue ink.

His legs felt weak as he walked toward Mitchell's office. She wasn't there. For a split second, he thought about slipping it under her door, but something stopped him. He saw

Carver's light was on in his office down the hall. He gently tapped on the door and saw Carver half asleep at his desk.

Carver smiled and waved Malone in.

"We really live here, don't we?" Malone said. "Want some coffee?"

"Yeah, we sure do," Carver said as he rubbed his eyes.

Malone stepped into the break room and quickly reappeared with two small cups of coffee. He handed one over to Carver, pulled the letter out from under his arm, and sat down. "Pull an all-nighter or something?"

Carver yawned out loud. "Nah, just came in extra early. Brass wants more dope on the table. Ya believe that?"

Malone could tell Carver was lying. He never went home. Malone also noticed Carver's speech was a little slurred. Not a lot, but enough that he knew it was there. Malone sipped his coffee.

"I sure do. What else is new? Like you can just make dope appear out of nowhere like a magic trick, huh?" Malone shook his head in disgust.

Carver nodded and then took a sip of his coffee.

"Assholes. Wouldn't be surprised if at some point they just tell us to pull drugs out of evidence for the photo ops," Carver cracked.

"Shit, I thought that's what they'd been doing for years," Malone said.

"What's up with the paper in your hand? You throwing in the towel?" Carver said with a small smirk.

"Yeah. I'm done. It's officially time to settle down." Malone handed the piece of paper over to Carver.

Carver's eyes widened as he read the page. "Really? You kidding? I was just joking."

He glanced it over and quickly handed the paper back.

"You're serious? Just like that? You're done?"

"Yeah." Malone sipped his coffee. "Just like that."

"Wait a minute," Carver interrupted and suddenly sounded like he sobered up. "I thought you said you wanted to come over to Narcotics?"

"I did. But I don't want to now. I can't do it," Malone replied.

"Malone, you know there ain't no switch you can just flip off and on like a light. Once a cop, always a cop. That's how it works." Carver stretched his arms out in the air and then folded his hands on the back of his head.

"Tell me—why you wanna do this right now?"

"It's just time," Malone replied.

"Just time? Wait. Wait a minute," Carver said and then looked at Malone hard for a moment. "You ain't gotta choice, right? Your wife—Ann—said you have to pick."

Malone nodded in agreement. "I do gotta pick. I pick them and I got three days to wrap up any shit here."

"Three days?" Carver smiled as he shook his head. He then brought his hands down to his desk and leaned forward in his chair. "You know that's a good reason to step down. But you know there ain't much you can do in a few days, other than wear yourself out. You're gonna find yourself in the damn hospital if you're not careful."

"I know, I know. But I'm gonna get Ace. That's gonna happen before I'm done," Malone said. "He ain't slipping away."

"You know all of CPD been looking for 'em for a few weeks now, ain't found him yet."

"Yeah. And that don't make sense. Unless..." Malone's voice trailed off.

"Unless what?"

"Unless he's getting help from someone on the inside."

"You've got to be kidding me. He killed two of our own, two police." Carver said.

"I know. Normally this bastard would have been behind bars in 48 hours."

Carver sighed and then frowned. "Man, you could be right. This is Chicago."

"Don't worry, I'm still gonna find this prick."

"Gotta admire your confidence."

Malone laughed. "Probably more stubbornness than confidence." He took the last sip of his coffee.

Carver laughed too. "I believe that. I believe that for sure."

Malone knew the coffee was waking up Carver now.

"Say you get your guy and you quit. What're things gonna look like down the road for you? Ride off into the sunset with your family?"

Malone put his hand on his chin feeling the stubble on his face.

"I dunno about that. But I'll have a family again. Finally get to spend time with my wife and kid."

"Yeah. But what are you gonna be like when you're with 'em? You ain't the type to just sit around watching cartoons and doing household chores, or joining your kid's PTO. Right? And I don't see you happy working in a cubicle or anything like that. You're a cop. Don't forget that."

Malone didn't respond.

Carver put his hands behind his head again. "I ever tell you I worked with your dad? Not directly, but I came across him a few times. You remind me of him a little bit."

"No," Malone said, as he leaned forward in the chair with wide eyes.

"Yeah, I did. Well, he was inching up to retirement, and I just got out of the academy. I once overheard him telling another officer that his biggest regret was that he didn't spend more time with you."

Malone put his hand on his mouth and moved it to his chin again. "Oh yeah? I never heard any of that before."

"And did your old man quit early to come home?"

"Nope. He didn't. He stayed until his ass was forced out by the brass."

"Right."

"And he didn't last long after he retired," Malone said.

"I don't want the same thing to happen to you," Carver said.

"Understood. Enough about me. How're you doing on this dope on the table deal?"

"Man, I ain't sure. Lots of leads, but not many people willing to knock on doors and hit the streets. Might be why I want your ass to join the team," Carver said.

"Rough, huh?"

"Yeah. Nothing changes. And that's what makes me think you ain't the only one thinking about hanging it up. But I got a feeling I'd go crazy with nothing to do. Going fishing'd get boring. I'd find myself watching cop shows while drinking too much. Before you know it, I'd be wishing I was back here in this chair."

"I could see you at a sporting goods store selling canoes," Malone cracked.

Carver laughed. "Selling tents and coolers, that kinda camping shit, eh?"

"You got your time in. Why not consider hanging it up?"

"Guess I ain't got nothing better to do. Old dog and all that." Carver finished his coffee.

Malone smiled.

"Now you think about what I said, will ya? At least come up with some kinda plan. No regrets. Your family deserves the best version of you possible."

"Yeah. You got a deal."

"Even if you are an asshole." Carver snapped.

Malone laughed and got up from his chair.

"Oh wait, I got something you need to know about," Carver said as he readjusted himself in his chair, sitting up straighter.

"Oh?" Malone was surprised.

"My CI told me she saw several big players from the Latin Kings and the Gangster Disciples meeting together."

"Bullshit. They hate each other. Been lighting each other up for years."

"Yeah. Maybe they've realized that less bodies means more profits and less police attention, right?"

Malone shrugged. "Where were they seen together?"

"Strip joint. Can't remember which one. Give Eve a call." Carver handed over a piece of paper with a phone number on it.

"Thanks." Malone stuffed the paper in the front pocket of his jeans. He shook his head in disbelief and started to walk to the door.

Carver stepped out from behind his desk and put his hand on Malone's shoulder. "Trust your gut. You'll make the right call with the job."

"Thanks."

"You're welcome. Now—"

"You don't gotta say it."

"I know. I know."

Carver nodded as he watched Malone leave his office. In a low voice, he said, "Watch your ass, Malone. Don't go off doing something stupid."

Malone stepped out of Carver's office feeling a bit better. He thought about something Carver said. It made good sense to have a plan. And he'd have to figure out this plan quick, the clock was ticking fast.

CHAPTER FIFTEEN

Malone got some coffee and then walked back to Vice. Mitchell still wasn't in her office. He entered the Vice office and saw Brown at his computer staring at some files.

"Hey, what's going on," Malone said as he sat down at his desk. Brown half waved and didn't say anything. "Hey, I ain't seen Mitchell lately, where is she?"

Brown shrugged. "I dunno. She said she was looking for you yesterday."

Malone looked back at his phone. He had another missed call from the same unknown Chicago number. This time they left a voicemail.

"Malone, it's Victoria Mitchell. Call me back."

Malone called the number back and stepped back into the hallway.

"Yeah, this is Malone."

"Malone, look, I know we got history, but I need you to do something for me."

"Oh?"

"Yeah, take over Vice for a while. I'm taking personal leave."

"Wait, you sure don't you want Ramirez for this? I just got back."

"I know. But I'm choosing you."

"Can I ask why, especially over Ramirez?"

"I know you'll get results. Ramirez won't get the same level of results you will."

"Thanks. Any idea how long you are taking off?"

"I'm not sure. My Dad's not doing well and needs a new liver. I really don't know how long this will be."

"Sorry to hear that," Malone replied. "Look, Lieutenant, I just don't know if I'm the right guy for the job."

"I wouldn't be offering it to you if you weren't. Higher ups will back me on this move too." Mitchell's voice was a bit shaky.

"Mmm-hmm."

"So you'll take the position?"

"Can you give me forty-eight hours? I need to talk to Ann first."

"Yeah, let me know. But Malone, please hurry."

"Will do."

Malone shook his head in disbelief as he went back in the office. "Hey, Brown."

"Yeah?" Brown turned to Malone.

"Where are we on some more prostitution stings?"

"Cole said he's meeting with his CI. I'm still sorting out some of the mess from the Marriott. They said there wasn't any more video."

"That's bullshit," Malone grumbled.

"Yeah, but they aren't giving me anymore."

"Have the girls who OD'd been identified?"

"Nope. Waiting on that."

"Who'd you talk to in crime lab?" Malone said as he took a sip of coffee.

"I can't remember. They said they were backed up."

"They always say that. Sometimes they need a little persuasion."

"Why does it matter?" Brown readjusted his glasses and leaned forward.

"I dunno. Just a hunch I guess. I'm thinking the drugs the girls overdosed on could be related to the drugs in shipped out from the warehouse I found yesterday."

"Maybe. Too bad about Lindsey."

"Yeah. Sure is." Just hearing her name pissed off Malone. He wanted Ace, right now.

Malone walked up to the front of the room, examining the photos on the wall. All of them were Latin Kings. He tried to remember everything that happened at the Marriott. Junior Garcia, Diego Gonzalez, Victor "King Bebo" Salazar, and Angel 'King L' Lopez.

He took a step back and looked at all of the names in front of him. He spent the next couple hours going over the files to look for anything he'd missed, and taking notes on everything he'd found on a yellow legal pad. He concluded that if the Latin Kings and Gangster Disciples were to suddenly start working together, it would probably be unofficial. Maybe a side hustle from someone wanting more cash on the side. Of the names in front of him, the most logical choice was Junior. Junior was the grandson of Ramon and with that came a hell of an ego. A known substance abuser, Junior also had a knack for making dumb decisions. Malone decided that he needed to find Junior and get him to talk about the drugs that killed the prostitutes.

He pulled up Junior's file on his computer and scanned it over. For the most part, he had never served any real time in prison. A few overnight stints, but that was about it. Junior had been known to be regular a massage parlor called Sunset Massage.

Ramirez entered the Vice office.

"Hey welcome back." Malone said.

"Thanks, doing good." Ramirez replied.

"Glad to hear it," Malone said slowly. It was going to piss off Ramirez that Mitchell chose him for the supervisor job. Malone ignored the thought. He had bigger things to worry about.

"Where are we on the girls from the hotel?" Ramirez said.

Malone hoped Brown would answer, but he knew he wouldn't. Brown wasn't going to say shit. Malone let the silence fill the room for a few seconds and then said, "I'm looking into a few leads from the Marriott. The girls that OD'd haven't been identified by the coroner yet, so we're focused on the guys who got away."

"Okay, good."

"But..." Malone said as he rubbed his hand on his chin.

"But what?" Ramirez said.

"I can't help but think this is tied to that drug warehouse yesterday."

"I heard about that but you have Latin Kings at the Marriott and Gangster Disciples at the warehouse. Tell me how any of that shit's tied together."

"Just a gut feeling. That warehouse was holding a shit ton of drugs. It's a goddamn distribution center."

"You know the administration just wants more prostitution arrests from us. They want us to focus our attention there, not drugs," Ramirez said.

"I know," Malone said, "and that's a major part of the fucking problem. All this shit is tied together like one giant knot."

"What are you doing now?" Ramirez leaned over and looked at Malone's computer screen.

"Looking into locations on the perps."

"Got anything?"

"Well, one of the men from the hotel, Junior, has been

known to be a regular at a massage parlor called Sunset Message. Thinking of going by there."

"Thought you were on desk duty, remember?"

"Fuck that. You and Cole were in the hospital because of these pricks," Malone said.

Ramirez shook his head in disgust and looked across the room at the whiteboard. "That all the guys from the hotel?"

"Yep. I put a star next to those who escaped. One in the middle is Junior."

Ramirez felt his chest with his hand and took a deep breath.

"A massage parlor," Ramirez mumbled to himself.

"You got the van?" Malone asked.

"Yeah, I got the van. Why? Is something wrong with your car?"

"I got a cruiser right now."

"What the hell happened to your car?" Ramirez said.

"Fender bender. But I'm fine. Got a new ride. That's all."

Ramirez looked at Malone like he was waiting for him to say something else.

"Where was this at?"

"Just down the road. By the library."

"What were you doing at the library?"

"No, I said *by* the library. I was on my way here and got sideswiped by an asshole. That's it."

Ramirez didn't respond.

Malone didn't care. He wasn't going to say it happened right by the bar. The library was about a block down further, but that was close enough.

"Brown," Ramirez said. "Send me the address. Malone, you stay here."

"What the fuck?" Malone said. "You're benching me now?"

"Mitchell did. Remember?" Ramirez said.

Malone sneered back and tightened his jaw.

"Want some backup?" Brown asked Ramirez.

"No. We're light on crew already. Keep digging up what you can on those girls from the Marriott," Ramirez said as he walked to the door and hurried out of the office.

Malone sat there at his desk for a couple minutes going through files and saw his reflection on the computer screen. "Want some coffee?"

Brown slowly shook his head no.

Malone walked to the break room. Just going past Carver's door reminded him of the CI, Eve. He pulled the piece of paper out of his pocket and dialed the number. It rang and rang. No response. Damn. He walked into the break room and the coffee pot was empty. He started a new pot and watched the coffee drip down slowly. This was bullshit. The clock was ticking. He wasn't going to sit around and wait. Fuck the chain of command.

Malone left headquarters and climbed into the cruiser and drove past Sunset Massage on Clinton Street. The massage parlor was a small rectangle-shaped space in an older beige brick strip mall with a green roof. Sunset Massage was located between a nail salon and a cell phone store, with a sub shop at the corner.

Malone had never been inside before, but just from driving by he knew it had to be really small. It looked like there was a lobby in the front and then a few separate rooms in the rest of the space. There were enough cars in the parking lot that the black police van didn't stand out. Malone parked the cruiser a block down on a side street and headed toward the massage parlor on foot. As he hurried down the street, he noticed a long brick building that looked like the back of an abandoned department store. He sneered as he saw the white lettering on the front of the building that read Chicago Fire Academy. He didn't hate fire as much as most other cops, but that didn't mean he was a fan either.

Once he arrived at the strip mall, he went into the sub shop at the corner and ordered a Coke. He sat down at one of the tables and sipped his drink as he watched the parking lot. Ramirez was still in the van, watching and waiting. There were only two entry points at the massage parlor: one in the front and one in the back. Malone then hurried out of the sub shop and snuck around to the back of the building. A row of dumpsters and access doors were in the back for deliveries.

Malone found the back door for the massage parlor. It was a thick gray door with minimal cover. On the ground, he saw some crushed cigarette butts. He didn't have time to wait around for another employee smoke break. He took a deep breath. Fuck it. "Delivery," he yelled as he knocked on the door. Nothing. Shit. He tried again, this time yelling louder and banging harder on the door. The door slowly opened, and Malone grabbed the door. A middle-aged Latino woman with black hair and glasses screamed, but not loudly. Malone barged into the hallway and the woman retreated back in fear. "Chicago Police," Malone said quietly but firmly. "Where's Junior?"

"No sé."

"I said, where is Junior?" Malone growled as he got in the face of the woman.

The woman reluctantly pointed down the hallway.

"Which door?"

"Segunda."

Malone nodded and walked to the second door. He put his ear up to the door and heard some moaning. He then promptly opened the door, with his P226 in hand.

Inside the small room, a naked woman with dark hair rocked back and forth on top of a man on a massage table in the middle of the room. Her body prevented Malone from seeing the face of the other person. The woman turned and let out an ear-piercing scream.

"Freeze! Hands up!" Malone barked.

The woman complied and raised both hands toward the ceiling.

"Get off of him. Now!" Malone said quickly.

The woman immediately got up and covered herself with a white towel as she moved off of the table. Malone could now see Junior lying on the table.

"What the hell, man? What the fuck you want?" Junior said as he leaned up on his side. He was completely exposed on top of the white blanket on the massage table. He sounded high or drunk. Maybe both.

Malone noticed some white powder on a mirror next to him on top of a small side table across from room. Under the table was a neatly folded stack of towels.

"We gotta talk. Now," Malone said.

Junior didn't reply.

"You can go," Malone said to the woman. The woman left the room and closed the door.

"Don't you fucking move," Malone said to Junior. "Put your hands up!"

"Man, fuck you," Junior said, ignoring Malone's order.

"Excuse me?" Malone said, "I said put your fucking hands up!"

Junior slowly raised his hands.

"A little cranky I interrupted, eh? Tell me what I wanna know or the next time someone's on top of you'll be at Cook County," Malone said with a smile.

Junior smiled back.

Malone noticed the gauze dressing on Junior's injured ear that Cole had shot.

"Tell me what I wanna know, and I won't arrest you," Malone said.

"Man, I ain't telling you shit."

"Your ear looks like it hurts," Malone said.

Junior's eyes widened. Malone stepped forward. Junior flinched and almost fell off the massage table.

Malone kept his P226 pointed at Junior.

"You can't shoot me, you're a cop. You got rules."

Malone smiled. "Who gave you the shit for the girls at the hotel?"

"Screw—you." Junior blurted out.

"Is that right?"

Malone pressed the gun harder below Junior's waist.

Junior groaned loudly in pain.

"You know, I'm just getting started here. Who gave you the drugs?"

Junior's screams turned into whimpers.

"I want a name. Now."

"Shit, I can't—argh!" Junior said.

Malone stopped for a moment and looked Junior in the eye. "Better start talking if you don't wanna start pissing through a tube."

"Look, I dunno his name."

"Bullshit!" Malone yelled and then he brought down the gun again, pistol-whipping Junior in the crotch.

Junior continued to scream.

"I don't like repeating myself. Gimme a name. Now."

"I don't got a name. But I think he could even be a cop. He leaves shit at drops for me."

"Stop spinning that bullshit story. I ain't buying. Why would a cop give you drugs?"

Malone noticed Junior was scared to look at him. He was sweating and shaking. His voice trembling, he said, "I dunno, man. I call a number and then I got drugs at drops all over the city. That's it."

Malone sighed out loud and then punched Junior in the

nose.

"Hurts like hell, doesn't it? Fucks you up. Your eyes start watering, your nose starts bleeding, your lungs crying out for air. And the whole time your brain is rattling in your skull wondering what happened."

Blood dripped off Junior's nose onto the five-point crown tattoo on his chest. Junior wiped his nose with his hand and the blood smeared across his face. Seeing the blood on his hand made him wish it was Malone's blood. His nostrils flared and his eyes widened.

Malone got closer and leaned over in front of Junior's face.

"Fuck you. Like I said, I ain't saying shit." Junior smiled, despite looking like hell.

Malone smiled back. "Always gotta be the hard way, huh?" He pistol-whipped Junior in the injured ear with his gun.

Junior groaned loudly in pain.

"You know, I'm just getting started here."

Junior's screams turned into whimpers.

"Gimme a name. Now."

"Shit, I can't—argh!" Junior said.

Malone jammed his P226 into Junior's stomach. "Feel that? I'm thinking about pulling the trigger and doing everyone a big favor. One less piece of shit drug dealer on the street."

"I'm—gonna—kill—you," Junior said through his teeth.

"Yeah, yeah, yeah." Malone slammed the gun down again, this time grip first. "You know, I don't enjoy this shit. I just want less dope on the streets. Fewer bodies. It's that simple, you know? If I gotta beat on you until that happens, guess that's how it's gotta be."

A loud thud came from behind Malone as the door flew open. Ramirez was at the door with his Glock drawn.

"CPD—freeze!" Ramirez barked out.

Malone saw Ramirez and said, "I'm just working on getting some info from this asshole."

"No. Stop. Now," Ramirez said firmly.

Malone looked back. "What the fuck are you—"

"Stop now! This asshole is under arrest."

Malone ignored Ramirez and readied himself to hit Junior again. "Who gave you the shit?"

Junior didn't respond.

"Malone, step back now. Don't make me take you down," Ramirez said.

"What the fuck? This shit bird and his crew shot at *both* you and Cole. He damn near killed you. Remember?"

"No more. He's under arrest."

"The hell he is. This asshole's gonna tell me what I wanna know," Malone said to Ramirez.

"Who's your supplier?" Malone screamed in Junior's face.

Junior smiled despite being in pain. "Go fuck yourself."

Malone went to hit Junior, but Ramirez grabbed Malone from behind and tried to knock the gun out of Malone's hand. Malone resisted, and swung his arm up, hitting Ramirez in the face with the side of the revolver.

"Fuck off," Malone barked. "This asshole is about to give up his supplier." Ramirez charged back at Malone and slammed him into the wall. Malone dropped the gun.

Out of the corner of his eye, Ramirez saw Junior had moved off of the table.

"Stop! Don't move!" Ramirez said as he picked up Malone's gun off the floor.

Junior froze in place.

"Get dressed." Ramirez said firmly to Junior.

Junior slipped on a shirt and his pants, then Ramirez put him in handcuffs.

Malone sat up and glared at Ramirez. He wanted to rip Ramirez apart. "You know this asshole could probably lead us to the supplier who gave the shit to those girls that OD'd."

"Maybe so. But we gotta take him in for medical attention," Ramirez said. "No thanks to what you did to him here."

"Fuck that," Malone said as he got in Ramirez's face.

"You forgetting I outrank you? It's my rules. And I'm playing by the book."

"You can stick that book up your ass," Malone said to Ramirez as he led Junior out of the room. Malone growled and then flipped over the small table with the rest of the coke on top of it causing the white powder to form a small cloud in the room. As Malone went out the front door, he saw Ramirez and Junior drive off in the van. Malone stood there frozen in place. Both of his hands balled up into fists. The thought of that asshole being back out on the streets in a few hours made Malone wish he had just pulled the trigger.

Malone got into the squad car and put his hands on the steering wheel. He tightened his grip on the wheel until he felt the muscles tense up in his arms. He realized he was shaking the steering wheel and let go. Malone took another deep breath and looked at the clock radio. It read three o'clock. Ann would be home soon with James. Part of him wanted to follow Junior and keep pushing for info. At some point, if he could just get him alone, he knew Junior would talk. But would that happen? Unlikely. He lit a cigar, turned the key in the ignition, and drove down the road.

CHAPTER SIXTEEN

Malone got to the house and parked in the street. He walked into the house and went straight to the kitchen. "Hey, where's James?"

"In his room playing," Ann said as she shut the refrigerator door.

"Okay. We need to talk," Malone said in an uneven, rushed voice.

Ann sat down in a chair at the kitchen table.

Malone put his shoulder holster on the back of a chair and then put his jacket over it. Then he sat down across from Ann.

"What's going on?" Ann asked with wide eyes as she looked at Malone.

"Before I turned in my resignation this morning, I was offered a promotion. A desk job."

"Mmm-hmm," Ann said with a slight nod.

"I'd be the supervisor for Vice. Would be a huge pay increase too. Like I said, a desk job."

Ann sighed and then chewed her bottom lip. "So you're

saying that you now want to stay on. After this morning, you said you were resigning."

"Before I was offered this big promotion. But yes."

"I can't believe you. Then again, I should know better," Ann said in a quiet voice like she was talking to herself.

"Hold up, hold up. This is bullshit. I can't make you happy no matter what I do," Malone said.

"Look, I *know* you. If you take that job, you'll want to go back out there. Maybe not at first, but soon you'll be neck deep in it again on the streets. You can't help it."

Malone sighed. "I'm telling you this a *supervisor* position. No field duty. A helluva lot more money too. We can get a bigger house in a nicer area, just like you wanted, remember?"

Ann shook her head no. "You're not *listening* to me. Stop being so goddamn stubborn and actually listen to me," Ann said. Tears swelled in her eyes.

"I'm listening to every word you've said. A few days ago, you were begging me to look at houses we couldn't afford. And with this promotion, we can now afford one of those houses. Remember?" Malone said.

"You say you're listening, but you're not. You promised you were out. And now you say you want to stay. I don't care what your job title is, or if you start wearing a suit or whatever. When something happens, you'll be back out there, getting shot at again."

"No, that's not true. Have you seen Carver? He—"

"No—you stay and you might as well sign your own death warrant," Ann interrupted.

"That's bullshit, and you know it." Malone raised his voice. Her words landed hard like a punch to the gut.

"It's not. I'm telling you the truth. It's time you accept it and stop lying to yourself," Ann said. She wiped tears from her eyes.

"Whatever." Malone suddenly got up from the chair and left the room.

"Where are you going?" Ann snapped.

"I'm gonna go see James. That okay with you?"

"Yeah. Of course."

Malone walked past the living room and up the stairs, noticing the photos hanging on the wall. Family photos from the past. James as a baby and a toddler. Going to Disney World a few years ago. Photos of another life. He flicked his eyes away from the wall and toward the top of the stairs. "Hey James, you there?" No response. Malone stepped closer. "You hiding?" Malone walked into his room and saw him on the floor lying face down. "Hey buddy, are you sleeping?"

Malone put his hand down and touched James on the shoulder. Nothing. "James. James?" Malone said in a shaky voice. He carefully turned James over and he was limp and unconscious. The blood froze in Malone's veins. James had blue lips and was not breathing. Malone wanted to scream, but the words wouldn't come to his lips.

He tried to check for a pulse and couldn't feel anything. He immediately knew what happened. He'd seen it countless times: a drug overdose.

Malone immediately started CPR. He counted out loud as he performed chest compressions. With each movement, Malone felt more numb. He had to pretend he was helping someone else to keep going. Then he got to thirty and performed two rescue breaths. James still wasn't breathing. "Fuck! No! No!" He hurried down the stairs and Ann met him in the hallway. "What? What is it?"

"Go start CPR on James. Now!" Malone screamed.

"What? Are you—"

Malone ran out the front door and pulled his phone out from his pocket. "My son stopped breathing. Likely overdose. I need an ambulance now. 5535 Elizabeth Street."

"Okay sir, help is on the way," the police dispatcher said.

"What's the ETA?"

"Just a couple minutes, sir."

Malone opened the door to the squad car and searched for some Narcan in the glove box. Nothing. He looked under the car seat. Nothing. Each passing moment felt like a countdown clock inside Malone's head and made him want to move faster. He ran around to the trunk. He found a first aid kit inside and opened it up. Bandages, gauze, medical tape, aspirin, ointment, a cold compress. "Motherfucker!" Malone ran back to the house and went upstairs. Ann was crouched over giving James more rescue breaths.

"The ambulance is gonna be here soon," Malone said. Ann didn't respond. Malone tried to see if James was moving at all now, but he looked the same. "Let me," Malone said. He continued doing CPR and James still wasn't responding. He counted out loud as he performed chest compressions. Malone heard sirens in the distance and ran back outside. Malone flagged down the ambulance and met them in the street.

"Need some Narcan now. Overdose. Give it to me. I'm a cop."

"Sir, we'll have to first—"

"Just gimme the fucking Narcan."

"Sir, wait a moment—"

Malone reached for his weapon, but it wasn't there. He remembered he left it inside the house.

"Fucking move it!" Malone barked.

The two EMTs nodded in agreement and followed Malone into the house.

"Excuse me, ma'am," one of the EMTs said. Ann reluctantly moved. The EMT kneeled down and started checking for a pulse.

Malone put his arm around Ann and noticed she was shaking.

"You hear me? It's a goddamn overdose!" Malone barked.

The other EMT handed over some Narcan and the one on the floor gave it to James.

Malone and Ann both watched and listened for any signs of James's breathing. Malone thought he heard something, but realized it was the sound of Ann breathing.

"Anything?" Ann asked the EMTs.

No one responded.

The EMT leaned over to see if James was breathing.

"I need the paddles."

The other EMT pulled out an orange rectangle-shaped defibrillator.

Malone fought the urge to look away. He pulled Ann closer and held her tight.

The EMT lifted up James' shirt and stuck the paddles on his chest. One of the paddles moved slightly on James. "Wait, wait. I've got some breathing here. Faint. Get me the BVM."

"Thank God," Ann said, as she hugged Malone.

Malone took a deep breath and nodded in agreement.

The other EMT handed over the bag-valve-mask. It was placed over James's mouth and nose. The EMT pressed the self-inflating bag and continued to check for a pulse. Then he took the BVM off of James. James coughed faintly, and then that cough sounded like snoring.

"Is he—he gonna be okay?" Ann said.

"Afraid it's too early to tell," one of the EMTs replied.

"He's gonna be fine," Malone said. "He's gonna be fine." Just seeing him breathing again meant the Narcan worked and he'd be okay.

The EMTs put James on a stretcher and started to take him out to the ambulance.

Malone's eyes flicked across the floor of James's room, and

he saw a small plastic bag by his son's feet. Malone's jaw tightened as he stepped forward and picked up the bag off of the floor and stuffed it in his pocket. He fought back the urge to scream and hurried down the stairs.

Ann was already in the back of the ambulance with an EMT, her eyes focused on James.

"Which hospital are you going to?" Malone asked.

"Holy Cross."

"I'll meet you there," Malone said.

Malone got into the police cruiser and scowled as he examined the plastic bag in his hands with orange, red, and green circle-shaped pills in it.

Malone pulled out his phone as he flew down the road.

Carver picked up on the first ring. "Yeah?"

"I got a big fucking problem," Malone said.

"What's the problem?"

"My...my son...fucking overdosed on something. Definitely an opioid. Was put on what looks like candy."

"Holy fuck. Is he okay?"

"Think so. I'm following the ambulance right now. Gave him some Narcan, and he's breathing."

"Thank God. I'll come to the hospital as soon as I can. In the middle of something."

"Okay. Holy Cross. Gonna need the lab to test this shit I found."

"Will do."

Malone hung up and wished he had a bottle of any kind of alcohol to help him calm down. Even some goddamn mouthwash would do right now. He tried to block out the heart palpitations and racing thoughts. James probably got the drugs from school. That definitely made the most sense.

Malone pulled into the parking lot and saw the ambulance unloading James and rolling him into the ER. Ann was right with James, holding his hand every step of the way.

Malone jogged to catch up with them. "Hey, Ann."

Ann slowly turned and looked Malone as they kept walking. Her eyes were bloodshot. She had a furrowed brow and said, "Huh?"

"He's gonna be okay. I know it," Malone said.

Ann sighed and looked back at James. "I gotta call my mom."

"I'll call Sarah," Malone said.

The EMTs moved James to a hospital bed and left.

"Any luck?" Malone said, seeing that Ann wasn't on the phone.

"Yeah, she's going to come down pretty soon."

"You get ahold of Sarah?"

"No. But I left her a voicemail."

For the next few hours, Malone and Ann sat next to James in small chairs in a small ER room separated by curtains. Several different nurses came in and checked James' vitals.

"How's he doing?" Malone asked a nurse with short blonde hair.

"A doctor will talk to you in a few moments."

Malone wanted to scream. That wasn't an answer. Both Malone and Ann waited together as there were a sea of voices and beeping sounds and footsteps passing by. Ann yawned and laid her head on Malone's shoulder as she watched James. Malone's phone rang. Carver. Malone carefully got up without waking Ann.

"Hey. I'm in the waiting room. I assume you're in the ER?"

"Yeah. I'll come to you." Malone said.

Malone hurried out of the ER, down the hallway and took a few turns and was in the waiting room. Tricia was sitting in the corner of the room. Carver was waiting by the door.

"How's he doing?" Carver said.

"Nobody's telling us shit, but I think he seems to be breathing a bit better."

"Well, that's good." Carver replied.

"Yeah." Malone reached into his pocket and handed over the plastic bag.

Carver looked at the bag. "I'll do whatever I can to get the results ASAP."

"Thanks. When James wakes up, hopefully he can give us more info."

Carver nodded. "You okay?"

"I'm not sure," Malone said. "It's like living in a nightmare. I keep hoping I'll wake up and things will be better."

"I'm sure." Carver put his hand on Malone's shoulder. "You know you got a tough one there. That Irish stubbornness. He's gonna be fine. He's just like his old man."

"Naw, he's a helluva lot better," Malone said with a smile.

Carver smiled too and started to walk away.

"Hey, I almost forgot," Malone said.

Carver turned around. "Yeah?"

"You mind contacting his school? Just in case. John Smyth on 13th."

"No problem. I'll talk to the principal."

"Thanks."

Carver left and Malone sat down next to Tricia.

"Hi Tricia," Malone said.

"Do you have any news?" Tricia asked.

"He's in stable condition right now. I can take you to him if you'd like."

"Absolutely," Tricia said.

"Okay."

Malone walked Tricia back to the ER. He couldn't help

but stretch his neck and shoulders over his head as he walked. Sitting in an uncomfortable chair for hours wasn't doing him any favors. He gently opened the curtain. Ann was watching James sleep. Tricia leaned over and kissed James on the cheek. Malone sat down in the empty chair and watched James. He wrapped both of his hands around James' small hand. Tears swelled in his eyes as he watched his son rest. After about a half an hour, Tricia went back to the waiting room.

A bald doctor with small glasses and a brown mustache appeared behind Malone and startled him. "Sorry to frighten you. I just was coming by to look at uh," the doctor said as he looked down at the file in his hand. "James. Just to see how James is doing."

"I'm Ryan, and that's Ann."

"I'm Dr. Shawn Carothers," he said with a nod and a slight smile.

Malone stepped to the side and got out of the doctor's way. The doctor looked back down at the file and then checked James' breathing.

"We're going to continue to aid your son's breathing and I'd like to start giving him fluids through an IV. I'd also like to do a blood test."

"Sounds good," Ann said.

"Yeah, for sure." Malone replied.

"I really think he's going to turn the corner here," Dr. Carothers said, "but we'll just have to wait and see. I'll get you moved over to your own room as well."

Dr. Carothers left and closed the curtain behind him.

Malone followed him out. "Excuse me, doctor," Malone said. "I'm a cop. I believe my son had a fentanyl overdose. Someone put it on some candy or gave him drugs that looked like candy."

"I was thinking that as well," Dr. Carothers said. "How long was he not breathing?"

"I'm not sure. We gave him Narcan as soon as the para-medics got there."

Dr. Carothers put his hand on his chin and in a dry tone said, "Well, you're doing all you can do. We should know more in the next couple hours."

The words hurt Malone's ears. He clenched his jaw and bit his lip. Hurry up and wait was not what he wanted to hear. Narcan typically was a miracle drug of sorts. He'd seen it bring someone from near death to walking and talking in a matter of minutes. And here his son was lying still in a hospital bed with a damn machine helping him breathe.

About an hour later, James was moved to his own hospital room. A small, dated room where everything was in different shades of white, brown, or beige. A brown door, a brown floor. Beige chairs. A beige wall. Two white walls. White sheets, a white ceiling. Malone had fallen asleep and woke up using Ann's shoulder as a pillow.

Ann put her hand over Malone's and smiled. She remem-bered when she first met him. She was teaching and took her second graders on a field trip to the Lincoln Park Zoo. They were leaving the zoo on the school bus and the bus got a flat tire on La Salle Dr. near the Chicago History Museum. It was her first field trip. She was the only teacher on a bus filled with eight-year-olds, three parent volunteers, the bus driver, and herself. Malone was working patrol. He actually boarded the bus and told the kids silly jokes while they waited for help with the tire. Ann contacted Malone's supervisors and Malone asked Ann out for coffee.

"Hey," she whispered.

"How's he doing?" Malone wiped the sleep out of his eyes.

"Think he's definitely breathing better. And I saw him moving around some in the bed."

"Good. How are you?"

Ann sighed. "Probably about the same as you."

Malone smiled. "That's fair."

"I just—I can't believe we almost—"

"Yeah," Malone replied slowly. "I can't either."

"My mom just went to get us some food."

"Great," Malone replied.

Dr. Carothers walked into the room.

"Got some good news and some bad news," Dr. Carothers said flatly.

The tone of how the doctor said that made Malone seriously wanted to punch him in the face.

"What's the good news?" Ann said.

"His vitals look good. I'm thinking in a few hours we can have the ventilator removed."

"The bad news?" Malone asked quickly.

"We're just going to have to keep a close eye on him for a while."

"That's it?" Malone straightened himself in the chair.

"Yes. Looks like he's going to make a full recovery." The doctor left the room.

"Great." Ann leaned forward and squeezed James' hand. Malone let out a sigh of relief and pulled his hands down his face.

Malone stepped out of the hospital room and called Carver.

"Hey, it's me. James is doing better, got his own room, and they're talking about taking him off the ventilator. Say he'll make a full recovery," Malone said in an unsteady voice.

"That's great," Carver said.

"Yeah, sure is."

"I'll come back down again as soon as I can."

"Good. You hear anything?"

"Afraid not. Lab is backed up as always. I'll let you know the moment I find out anything."

"Okay."

"I did talk to the principal as well as James's teacher. They're contacting all of the parents. I'll let you know if anyone contacts me."

"Good. Thanks."

"Why don't you go get some rest? You sound like you're half-awake."

Malone yawned and then laughed. "Yeah. Ain't easy in a hospital. I'm gonna stay here with Ann." Malone hung up and went back into James's room.

Ann was eating a sandwich and said, "Mom dropped off some food and went home to rest."

"Okay. I think I'll have something later." His eyes were heavy, and he collapsed in the chair next to Ann. He knew he couldn't sleep, but he closed his eyes.

He heard a familiar voice and opened his eyes. James was awake.

CHAPTER SEVENTEEN

Malone ran over to James and put his arms around him. He squeezed tight. For a while, it had felt like James wasn't going to make it.

"You're okay. I knew you'd be okay."

"Dad, you're squishing me," James said in a whisper.

"Sorry, pal. Just so glad to see you. I love you so much."

Malone woke Ann, who jumped out of her chair and kissed James on the cheek and then again on the head. "How are you feeling?"

"My—uh—stomach feels funny. Like I gotta throw up," James said quietly.

"It'll feel better soon, I know it," Ann said.

"Where are we?" James asked as he looked around the room.

"We're at the hospital, pal," Malone replied.

"Oh," James said. "Why?"

"I think you took something that looked like candy, but it wasn't."

"You mean the little bag of candy I had?"

"Yes, exactly. Where'd you get the bag from?" Malone said.

"I got it from Jacob. In my class. Some older kid gave it to 'em." James replied.

Malone turned to Ann. "Do you have the number for Jacob's parents?"

"Yeah, I'll call them right now."

Malone nodded in approval.

"Did you see who gave the bag to Jacob?" Malone asked.

"Yeah, but I never seen him before." James replied.

"But you can remember what he looks like?"

"I think so."

"Good. Do you remember anything else?"

James sniffled and quietly said, "They drove a black truck with shiny gold wheels."

"Did you see who drove the truck?" Malone asked.

"Yep. I saw him."

"Good. Do you think any of the other kids in your class or your teacher saw this truck or the people that gave him the bag?"

"I dunno." James shrugged.

"Okay. You did great," Malone said.

"That's gonna help you catch the bad guy?"

"Yeah, I think it will." Malone said, as he gave James a big hug and held him tight. "I'm gonna get him, buddy. Believe me, I'm gonna get 'em."

Ann got in touch with Jacob's parents and thankfully Jacob forgot about it and never touched the candy. Jacob mentioned to his parents that he saw a black truck as well.

Ann found some old cartoons on television and it was great to see James smile as he watched. Ann wrapped her hand Malone's and squeezed. She looked over at him and felt better until she saw the scowl on his face. He wasn't really there. In his mind, he was already out on the streets hunting down whoever was responsible for what happened to James.

Malone flinched when he heard the sound of his phone ringing. It was Carver. He stepped out of the room.

"Yeah?" Malone rubbed his eyes.

"Just got the results from the lab. On that candy was a unique mixture of both meth and fentanyl."

Malone felt his heart in his throat. He tried to squeeze out some words, but they wouldn't come. He clenched his jaw and fought the urge to put a hole in the wall with his fist.

"Malone?"

Malone didn't respond and kept his eyes on the floor.

Carver leaned forward and said, "Malone, these drugs were made using the same process as the chemicals at the warehouse."

Malone felt his gut sink. "Any—uh—any fingerprints on the bag or the pills?"

"A few partials, but nothing we can use."

"Can you bring me some photos? I think James may be able to ID who gave him the drugs."

"Yeah, I'll send someone down with some photos."

"Thanks." Malone hung up and kissed James on the cheek. "How are you feeling?"

"Still kinda fuzzy."

"Can I get you some food or something? Maybe even a smoothie?"

"I'll take a smoothie!" James said excitedly.

"I'll be right back." Malone went down to the cafeteria and walked past the other food toward the drinks and found the smoothies. He got a large peanut butter smoothie and went his way back to James' room.

Ann had her arm around James in the hospital bed.

"Well, look at this, you brought me a milkshake?" Ann said in a playful tone.

"Oh no, this is for me. You want one, you're on your own," Malone said as he pretended to drink from the red straw in the white cup.

"Hey," James said.

"Just kidding. One peanut butter smoothie as requested." Malone handed James the drink and he immediately took a big sip.

Brown knocked on the hospital room door. "Malone?"

"Yeah?"

"I got some photos for you." He gave Malone a manila folder that was closed with a paperclip.

"Great, thanks."

"I got these from Carver," Malone said to Ann. "I think James may be able to ID who gave him the—uh—plastic baggie."

Ann nodded slowly, cautiously.

"Are you sure he's up for this?"

"Yeah, I am. I really think he can do it."

"Okay, then let's do it," Ann said. James was half asleep, but Ann woke him up.

"Hey pal, can you help me out with something?" Malone asked.

James was looking around, clearly groggy, but shook his head yes.

"Okay, I've got some pictures for you. I want you to tell me if you recognize any of these guys, okay?"

Malone sat next to the bed and opened the file folder. He held up gang member photos one at a time in front of James. A mixture of Gangster Disciples, Latin Kings, and Vice Lords. Nothing. Then he held up Shorty's photo.

"Yeah, he's the one that gave Jacob the baggie."

"Are you sure?"

"Yep. He was wearing a black White Sox shirt like the photo."

Malone swallowed hard and then coughed lightly to distract himself. "Okay, that's good pal." He continued to flip through the photos. Ace's photo was next in the stack, and Malone's hand shook slightly as he held it up.

"Yep—he was driving the black truck."

Malone swallowed hard. "Are you sure?"

"Yep. That's who I saw."

"Okay. That's really good." Malone stood up immediately and said, "I'll be back as soon as I can. Love you."

Ann got up from her chair and stood in front of Malone, looking him in the eye. "I know you gotta go, but be careful. We need you back..." Ann's voice trailed off as she covered her mouth to hold back her tears. "You hear me?"

"Yeah. And then I'm done." Malone said.

Malone hurried out of the hospital into the night. He climbed into the Crown Vic and sped down the dark road. He flipped on the siren to move the other cars out of the way and zoomed through all of the lights. His thoughts came together to focus on Ace and nothing else. He wasn't getting away with this shit. He wasn't going to keep doing what he'd been doing. No more slaps on the wrist. This fucker needed to face real justice, once and for all.

He turned off the siren and parked the police car on the street down a block from the pool hall. Malone walked into the pool hall without body armor or back up. He didn't care how many were inside. He just wanted Ace. Nothing else mattered. He stuffed his handgun into his jacket pocket, hiding most of it, other than a part of the grip. Slowly, he walked into the pool hall, ready for anything. The building was mostly a bar with six pool tables to the right filling up the space. The bar was busy with both men and women sitting on the stools chatting and drinking.

Malone walked toward the pool tables. Two large Black men with pool cues in their hands stood in the way. Malone didn't say anything, leading to a moment of uncomfortable silence. Finally, Malone said, "I heard this place has good chicken wings. That true?"

"You heard wrong. Get the hell outta here," the man on the left said. He had a large gold chain with the star of David on it, the symbol of the Gangster Disciples.

"Shit, I bet you like chicken wings almost as much as you do Latin King ass."

The man lunged forward at Malone, swinging his pool cue at Malone's head.

Malone quickly stepped to the side and then pistol-whipped the man in the back of the head. The man crashed into a nearby table, sending some drinks flying. Then the man fell to the floor, out cold.

Malone pointed his P226 at the other man.

"Before you get any bright ideas, it ain't smart assaulting a police officer."

"Man, fuck you," the other man said.

"You're not my type. Got a feeling you might be his type though," Malone pointed back with his thumb at the other man on the ground.

"Where's Ace?"

"Huh?"

"I get pissed when I gotta repeat myself. You heard me."

"I dunno no Ace."

"Right."

Malone watched the man's eyes move across the room. The man suddenly stepped forward and threw a punch at Malone. Malone took it in the jaw, picked up a beer bottle, and broke it on the other man's head. The man crashed down to the ground holding his head.

"Thanks for all the help," Malone said, and left the man on the ground.

Malone saw Shorty come out of the bathroom. He was wearing large gold chain and a White Sox t-shirt.

Shorty smiled at Malone and pulled the fire alarm.

Everyone inside started running towards the exits. Malone fought his way through the crowd, but Shorty had already escaped. "Fuck!" Malone screamed and then shook his head in disbelief.

Malone paused by the bar and noticed the bottles glistening under the lights. A drink would take the edge off a little. Malone quickly turned his head away and walked toward the front exit.

"Ryan Malone?"

Malone turned back to see a black man in his early thirties with a shaved head and a stubble beard. His name popped into Malone's head.

"Kevin," Malone said. "Kevin Porter. How are you? I ain't seen you in years. What's it been?"

"Probably ten years, easy. Maybe more. Can't believe it's you. How the hell are you?" Porter said.

"Well, I was after a perp in here. The asshole pulled the fire alarm to get away."

"Don't give me that, I saw you come in stirring up trouble."

"Who me?" Malone smiled. "Wait, you work here?"

"Yeah, been here part-time for last few months. I help with inventory, keep the bar stocked, whatever is needed, really."

"Nice. How's your brother, Jesse?"

"Good. Got a wife and kids now. Lives north of town in one of those fancy suburbs."

"Where's he working?"

"ATF, I think. You see anyone from the old neighborhood or from high school?"

"Not lately. Just been neck-deep fighting this shit storm,

you know? Speaking of which, you know a guy named Ace? I'm looking for him. He's one of the many Gangster Disciples around here."

Porter shook his head no. "I dunno him, but I bet I know someone who does. Follow me."

Malone followed Porter into the night and they walked past a barbecue joint and small convenience store. "How you been?" Malone asked.

"Not bad. Just weird being in the States instead of being stationed in Afghanistan. All they got over there is sand, man."

"Safe to say you ain't going to the beach anytime soon, huh?" Malone said.

"Hell no," Porter replied with a chuckle. "How 'bout you? How the hell are you still working for the CPD?"

"Being a cop ain't the problem. It's the assholes that get in the way."

"Could stitch that on a throw pillow, you know?"
Malone smiled.

"Here we go," Porter said as he walked into a parking lot of a storage facility.

Malone was a little surprised it was there. This neighborhood had mostly locally owned family businesses. One after another.

"Jeez, these damn places are everywhere," Malone said.

"Gotta have a place to store your stuff," Porter said. "Good business model, always in demand."

"But what are we doing here?"

"I'll show you." Porter kept walking.

The storage facility was made of two long narrow rows of garage-like buildings that stretched back as far as the eye could see. "Tell me this ain't no damn scavenger hunt," Malone said as he saw the long stretches of buildings.

"Hell no. Have some faith, man."

Porter led Malone around the office for the storage facility. Right behind there was a small space between the two buildings and a dumpster for cardboard.

"Hey, Devon, you there?" Porter called.

An older black man in his sixties with gray hair and a thick bushy gray beard popped his head out from behind the dumpster. His eyes were heavy, and he rubbed them as he looked up at Malone and Porter.

"Huh? Who'd there?"

"Hey Devon, it's me. I got some food for you back at the bar."

"Thanks, man."

"Also want you to meet a friend of mine. He's got a question for you."

Devon stepped out around the dumpster, eyed Malone, and looked back at Porter.

"This is Malone. Good guy. Well, most of the time," Porter said with a chuckle. "Needs a little help."

"Ain't nothin in this world totally free," Devon said.

Malone snickered and pulled out a twenty-dollar bill from his faded leather wallet. He handed it over to Devon.

"I'm looking for Ace. Know where I can find him?"

"Ace? Hmm. Yeah, I know him. Tattoo on his neck, right?"

"Uh-huh. Where can I find him?"

"I dunno. Maybe he's staying at his girl's?"

"You shitting me?" Malone leaned forward. "That all you got?"

"I dunno nothing else. Ain't seen him around in a while."

Malone sighed. "What the hell did I just pay for, man?"

Porter stood in front of Malone. "It's okay, man. It was worth a shot. Right?"

"Yeah, you're right. Let me know if you see him?" Malone held out one of his business cards.

"Yeah. Sure," Porter said.

Malone shook Porter's hand. "Thanks. Good seeing you."

On his way back to his car, Malone called Eve. This time, she picked up.

"Hey, it's Ryan Malone. Carver gave me this numb—"

"Yeah. Make it fast. I can't talk long," Eve said quietly.

"Does Ace have a girl he'd stay with?"

"I'm not sure. I ain't seen him with a girl."

"Anything. Anything at all could help me out here."

Eve snapped her gum as she thought for a minute. "Lemme call you back." She hung up.

Malone sat alone in the car and put his hands on his face. Every choice he made had led to nowhere. It was hard to breathe, hard to function. Nothing but hitting one dead end after another. He didn't have any other choice. Malone got out of the cruiser and stood on the sidewalk where the brisk air hit him in the face. He flicked on his flashlight and cut into the cold, dark alleyway.

CHAPTER EIGHTEEN

It probably was a bit of a long shot, but Malone had the feeling that Shorty was still nearby. He searched the area for the next half hour, but found nothing. The pool hall was on the first floor. Some apartments were on the second and third. He heard footsteps and flipped off his flashlight. Didn't want to scare off anyone. More footsteps. A man's voice was getting louder. He was singing. The streetlight overhead revealed a drunk holding a bottle of malt liquor. The man kept walking down the alley and disappeared.

"Screw this," Malone mumbled to himself. He went back into the pool hall. It was mostly empty.

Porter was working behind the bar and nodded his head at him. "Decided to come back for more, did ya?"

"I'm thinking the perp I saw earlier might come right back here. Not the brightest bulb, you know?"

"Yeah. Wouldn't surprise me at all. Want a beer or something?"

Malone exhaled. "No thanks, I gotta keep a clear head. Some club soda or something like that would be fine, though."

"Sure thing."

Porter walked to the other end of the bar and came back with a clear glass for Malone.

"What the hell are you really doing working here?" Malone asked before he took a sip.

"Change of pace, I guess. Something different. I mean, sure, we get some fights and some shit in here, but it's nothing like overseas. No IEDS, not too many fuckers with AK47s gunning for me here."

Malone smiled and held back his laughter until he saw Porter chuckle.

"With your skills, man, you could really put them to use."

"You mean join the force?"

"I dunno. Maybe. Even in a suburb. Glenview, Naperville, some shit like that."

"I'm done taking orders from anyone, you know?"

"I can respect that." Malone took a sip of his drink. "Maybe you could do some freelance."

"Maybe. Until then, here I am."

Malone slipped off to use the men's room. Standing by the urinal, he couldn't help but realize how tired he was. He shook off the feeling and decided to ignore it. As he washed his hands, Porter opened the door.

"You called it, man. That little asshole came back. Playing at one of the back tables. Brought more guys with him too."

"How many we talking?"

"Three."

Malone's eyes glanced toward the bar and then back to Porter.

"You got a gun here?" Malone asked.

"Yeah, a shotgun behind the bar."

"Get it. I'm gonna run him out the back door."

"How you doin' that?"

"I'll figure something out."

"All right." Porter opened the men's room door and Malone followed him out with his P226 at his side and kept his head down. Thankfully, the lighting was dim and the men were distracted playing pool. Malone watched Porter, who nodded his head once he had the shotgun.

Malone glanced up and saw Shorty with three other men he didn't know.

"Freeze! You're under arrest, asshole," Malone said as he pointed his P226 at Shorty.

Shorty laughed as three other men reached for their guns.

"Don't even try that shit," Malone turned toward the other men and Porter appeared with the shotgun. "Put your guns on the table." The three men listened and slowly put their guns on the pool table.

Shorty ducked out the back exit.

Malone hurried after him. Gunfire rang out toward Malone in the alley. It sounded like a 9mm. It was too dark to see anything without a flashlight. Shit. He found some cover behind a trashcan. The gunfire stopped. He flicked on the flashlight and saw Shorty running down the alley. Malone hurried and soon caught up with him. Malone screamed, "Freeze! Don't move! Show me your fucking hands!"

Shorty stopped but didn't put his hands up, keeping them in front of his body. "Put your hands up. Now!"

Shorty glanced back at Malone.

"Don't do it," Malone said under his breath. "Don't you fucking do it."

Shorty suddenly turned around with his 9mm raised and Malone fired his P226, hitting Shorty in the chest. Shorty fell down, dropping the gun.

Malone hurried over and holstered his weapon. "Where's Ace?"

No reply. Malone hovered over Shorty and kept the flashlight in Shorty's face. "I said, where's Ace?" Malone screamed.

Shorty coughed. He struggled to breathe.

"You ain't dead, you stupid fuck. I know you hear me. Tell me and I'll get you help."

"Fuck. You." Shorty gasped.

"That how it's gonna be?" Malone growled.

Malone picked up Shorty's 9mm off the ground. "Tell me where Ace is, right now, or say bye bye. You give kids—my kid—poison."

Shorty laughed. "Well, fuck you. And fuck your kid too," Shorty said. "Money's money."

Malone held the pistol to the side of Shorty's head and pulled the trigger. The sound of gunshot echoed in the alleyway and blood splattered on the concrete.

He looked down at the body on the ground and took a deep breath. He felt nothing. No pleasure, no pain, no relief, no remorse. Nothing. It had to be done. If anything, he was pissed that he couldn't get any information from him. His instincts made him want to call in the shooting, but he refused to stand around for a few hours filling in paperwork. Fuck it.

Malone wiped down the 9mm for prints and tossed it into a dumpster. He turned left to go back to the pool hall. He found Porter lying holding his stomach on the floor. Fuck. He was groaning out loud. Clearly, he'd been beaten up pretty good.

"You okay, man?" Malone said as he helped Porter up.

"Some more fuckers came in and attacked me all at once."

"They didn't shoot you or anything?"

"No, but I think one of those assholes was wearing steel-toed boots. Or dropped a bowling ball on my gut."

"Shit. Sorry, man," Malone said. Malone noticed Porter had a cut on his forehead.

"I can take you to the hospital," Malone said. "That cut looks pretty bad."

"I guess, okay."

Malone and Porter got into the police cruiser. Malone started the car and his phone rang.

"Malone? It's me," said Eve. "I may have something useful. I think Ace could be with Tasha Brown. Lives on the Northside, 3232 Wilton."

"No shit," Malone replied. "Thanks."

"Sure," Eve said.

He typed on the computer and found the details for Tasha Brown. No criminal record. Malone noticed she had a newer red Civic in her name too. Malone knew he didn't have time for a stakeout. He needed results. Now.

"I may have a lead to check out. You up for it or want me to take you back?" Malone asked.

"I'm in. Let's go."

"You sure? You kinda look like shit."

"That ever stop you?" Porter snapped.

"You got a point there. You can back me up, okay?"

Porter nodded. "Shit, I already had your back just a minute ago. Didn't I?"

"You did. Other than getting your ass kicked, you did pretty good," Malone smiled.

"You're gonna get me back into fighting shape, eh?" Porter said.

"You know I will," Malone said with a smile.

CHAPTER NINETEEN

Malone parked a few blocks away from Tasha Brown's townhome. It started to snow and the streets were quiet.

"Man, that cop car sure ain't you," Porter said as he walked next to Malone.

Malone laughed. "Yeah, I know. Borrowed it from a friend. Beats walking."

"And yet, here we are walking around in the fucking cold," Porter said.

"Man, you did get soft. Here you are whining at me," Malone replied.

Porter laughed. "Chicago is a helluva lot colder than Afghanistan."

"You got a point there."

Malone saw a black truck with tinted black windows parked on the street. He flicked on his flashlight and saw the gold rims. "Here you are, you piece of shit."

"What are we up against here?" Porter said.

"A sick fuck who gives kids drugs and kills cops. That's what."

"I see. And you want me to help keep an eye out?"

"Yeah. Do you need another gun?" Malone asked.

"No, I'm good with this," Porter held up the shotgun.

"Okay good. Think that's his girl's place there," Malone motioned to the townhome up a short concrete stairway. "And that black truck matches the description of Ace's vehicle. The red Civic is Tasha's."

"Enough said. Just like junior high, right?" Porter replied with a smile.

"Yeah. Go ahead," Malone handed his flashlight over to Porter.

Without hesitation, Porter smacked the side of the door hard. The flashlight bounced back onto the sidewalk. The car alarm blared and the lights flashed.

A woman in a pink robe came to the front door and turned off the alarm with a button on a remote. Malone and Porter both stayed in position out of sight and waited. The woman didn't come outside.

They watched her as she stood there in the doorway. Finally the alarm stopped, and she closed the door.

Malone gestured to Porter to do it again. Porter took the flashlight and hit it on the door, setting off the alarm once more.

Tasha opened the door and a male voice screamed from inside. It was unclear who it was or what was said. The alarm stopped again. Malone looked over at Porter. "I'm gonna go around back," Malone whispered.

Malone went around back and quietly moved past the garage, entering the back yard. The lights were on in the townhome, but no one could be seen walking around inside.

As Malone approached, he pulled out a pair of black gloves from his pocket and slipped them on. Malone drew his revolver from the waist of his jeans and kept moving. He noticed his heart beating faster. A dog started barking loudly a couple houses over. He tried to ignore it, but the barking got louder. Then he heard a familiar voice scream, "Shut yo' damn dog up!" It was Ace.

Malone stopped at the wooden stairway that went up a flight of stairs to the back door. The dog's barking died down. Malone crouched and kept his eyes on the brick building.

There were six small windows, two on each floor. His eyes flicked quickly between the windows. His heart pounded harder in his chest. Instead of trying to shrug it off, he embraced it as a way to focus his attention into short bursts.

Malone looked up at the second-story window on the left and then the right. Thud. Then he shifted down to the first story, the left and right. Thud. When he made it to the end of the walkway, Malone stopped. Another townhome was nearby, just a few feet behind the townhome. If this asshole were to fire a weapon out the window, it could easily hit the neighbor.

He stayed there in position and listened carefully. The tapping of footsteps came from above. He pointed his P226 up and waited. His heartbeat shook his body in between breaths.

Exhale.

Thud.

Inhale.

Hold.

Thud.

Someone appeared on the back deck, holding what looked to be a shotgun. Malone watched and waited until the individual went back inside the townhome. He phoned Porter.

"Hey. Got someone on the second floor with a shotgun. Just went back inside."

"You wanna call for backup?" Porter said.

"We get SWAT or more cops here, this ain't gonna get any better. Just a better chance more cops get hurt."

"We don't know if anyone else is in the building," Porter said.

"Exactly. Anyone comes running out the front, be ready."

"Shit, don't go in alone, man. Malone, you gotta wait—" Porter realized Malone had already hung up.

Malone slipped his P226 into his shoulder holster and pulled the revolver from waist. Slowly, he started up the creaky stairs. He had to end this. Now.

Malone couldn't help but think of James as he shifted his feet up the stairs. This was for him. He thought of Ann too. He even wondered about this girl who owned the townhome. Tasha probably didn't know much about Ace. He'd probably been telling her lie after lie. Hell, she probably thought he was a decent guy.

Now on the second floor, Malone pointed his gun at the door. Carefully, he tried the handle. It was unlocked. He readied himself and stepped through the white door. It led to the kitchen. Malone noted all possible threats and quickly checked them. Nothing to the left. Nothing to the right. Nothing in the corners.

His eyes shifted ahead to an island in the kitchen. A good place to take cover. Malone moved closer, ready to fire. He inched closer to the island and imagined Ace there on the hardwood floor, ready to spring up. The shotgun at this kind of range would mean game over. Malone moved slowly and focused each movement.

Ace was so close he could feel it. He wanted to pull the trigger and end it right now. He knew he was waiting right there. It made perfect sense. Malone saw something out of the corner of his eye and turned to his left one more time. From the angle, he could see the other side of the island. Ace wasn't there. He saw a bathroom to the right, then a dining room and living room on the other side. Malone picked up a full bottle of spaghetti sauce off the kitchen counter and threw it into the bathroom. Glass shattered loudly as it hit the tile floor.

Ace was sitting in the living room on the couch and grabbed his shotgun. He got up and saw Malone near the hallway and immediately fired the shotgun in Malone's direction. Malone dove to the kitchen floor, disoriented from the boom of the shotgun. He knew his hearing couldn't be trusted now. He used his phone as a mirror and saw Ace walking down the hallway toward him. Malone kept the phone steady and gritted his teeth as he waited. He was only a few feet away now. Malone had to remind himself to take a breath. Once he saw Ace, Malone ducked out and shot him in the right leg. Ace stumbled and fell to the kitchen floor but still held onto the shotgun.

"Drop it, asshole!" Malone barked.

Ace fired the shotgun at Malone from the ground, hitting the kitchen island. Malone crawled around to the other side of the island and fired at Ace again, causing him to run out of the room.

Malone reloaded the revolver and took a deep breath. He then carefully moved toward the living room using the wall for cover. Ace was there in middle of the room holding a shotgun on Tasha. Tasha was frozen with fear and her breathing was unsteady. Ace pointed the shotgun at the side of her head.

"Drop it, or I'll shoot her!"

Malone kept the revolver pointed at Ace. "Wait, you don't wanna do that," Malone said, "I'm gonna put the gun down." Malone suddenly fired the revolver, shooting Ace in the hand.

Ace dropped the shotgun and Tasha ran to the corner of the room.

In a split second, Malone was on top of Ace and pushing the revolver into Ace's forehead. "You like giving drugs to kids? You fucking piece of shit!"

"Man, I didn't force no one to take nothin."

"Right," Malone said, "You make me fuckin' sick." Malone punched Ace in the face. "You're gonna talk, you piece of shit. You hear me?" Malone pointed the gun under Ace's chin. "Feel that? Gonna be the last thing you ever feel."

Ace smiled and laughed.

"Something funny?" Malone pulled the gun away.

"Yeah. You full of shit."

"Is that right?" Malone said. Ace pulled a knife from his pocket and slashed Malone in his right forearm, causing him to drop his handgun. Ace tried to cut Malone again, but this time Malone was ready and knocked the knife away.

Malone leaned down to find his gun and Ace punched him in the face, hitting him in the eye. Then Ace picked up the shotgun, cracking Malone in the head with the butt of the weapon. The blow rattled his skull and made everything fuzzy. Malone fell to the ground.

"Get your ass up," Ace said.

Malone slowly stood up.

Ace pressed the shotgun against Malone's cheek. "This gonna be the last thing you ever feel."

Malone glared back at Ace's cold dark eyes. He refused to beg. He wouldn't do it, no matter what. Malone noticed the gun was shaking slightly and blood was dripping down Ace's right hand. Malone pulled his head back and hit the shotgun upward with his right arm, knocking the gun out of Ace's hands. Malone punched Ace in the gut and followed with another shot to his face. As he picked up the revolver from the ground, Malone growled. Malone pointed his gun at Ace. "You're done. Tell me who you're working with."

Ace smiled. "You ain't got nothing, man. I ain't sayin' shit."

"Right," Malone said.

Ace charged forward, grabbing at the handgun. He took a

swing at Malone face with his left hand, but Malone blocked with his injured forearm. Ace grabbed Malone's gun hand and locked it under his arm. He put his free hand on the revolver. Malone resisted and Ace pulled more on the gun.

A quick burst of shots rang out. Several rounds went into the ceiling. One into a chair. A couple at the couch. A round hit Tasha in the chest, and she slumped over. Ace grabbed at the gun again and it flew out of Malone's hand onto the floor.

Malone punched Ace in the stomach and then followed with a knee to the crotch, causing Ace to hunch over and step back. Malone threw a quick jab to the jaw and followed with another that clipped Ace in the cheek. Ace jerked his head back, tried to gather himself, and threw a wild jab to Malone's jaw with his bloody hand. The punch missed, and Malone tackled Ace to the ground. Once Ace was secure, Malone looked over at Tasha. She wasn't moving and her eyes had glazed over. She was gone.

Malone scowled and wrapped his hands around Ace's neck and started to squeeze, feeling the air go out of Ace's lungs. He squeezed harder until Ace started to pass out. Dropping him, Malone picked up his gun and pressed the barrel against Ace's forehead.

Ace just stared back and didn't say a word.

Malone knew he wasn't going to talk. Malone thought of James and Johnny and Leo. He saw Tasha's lifeless body out of the corner of his eye. He gritted his teeth and a sneer crept across his face as his eyes clouded up with tears. "Fuck you," Malone said as he pulled the trigger, shooting Ace in the head.

Finally, he felt some relief. He drew in a deep breath and slowly exhaled. A weight had been lifted and it was the first time he'd felt like himself in a long time.

As he stood there, he looked down at Ace's body on the floor. Then he turned and saw Tasha's body on the couch. She looked like she was asleep. Maybe passed out drunk or nodded off from a fix. But the blood covering her told another story. She wasn't breathing. She was gone, and Malone couldn't stop it from happening. Malone paused for a moment as he looked at Tasha. She looked younger. Maybe even like a teenager. Malone's stomach sank. He remembered he still had one more job to do and nothing was going to stop him now.

CHAPTER TWENTY

Porter waited outside the townhome and Malone slowly limped outside. Malone looked like shit and was holding something wrapped in a small blue towel with some blood on it.

"Hey. You okay? I heard some gunfire." Porter said.

"Yeah. I'm okay."

"Need to go to the hospital?"

"Did I say that I did?" Malone slowly limped to the police car and leaned on the trunk. "I'll be fine. This shit ain't over yet. Got one more thing to do. Then I'll go to the hospital."

"You gotta call this in? I heard gunfire."

Malone shook his head no. "This last thing and I'm done. I'm out."

Malone's head was throbbing like crazy, but his thoughts were moving fast. He opened the driver's door to the cruiser.

"Sure you're okay to drive?" Porter asked, as he rushed toward the driver's seat.

"What the hell, you drive."

"You getting smarter, ain't ya?"

"Don't feel too smart right now," Malone said as he lit his

last cigar. He pulled back the sleeve of his jacket and took a look at his arm. His arm was bleeding a little, but the blood had been soaked up by his black long-sleeved shirt.

"While you were inside, two Latino guys passed by the house."

"Get a look at 'em?"

"Not really. Too dark. One had a bag in his hand. Think they heard the gunshots and left. That's my guess."

"Anything else?"

"Shorter guy was limping pretty bad. Like he got messed up."

"Hmm." Malone's head was hurting too bad to think right now.

"Where we going?"

"Downtown. Take Wacker Dr."

"Sure."

"Thanks for helping me out." Malone said.

"No problem."

Malone chuckled lightly, then winced in pain. He reached into his jacket pocket and pulled out some ammunition for the revolver.

"I gotta say, I don't like the looks of this if you're gonna do what I think you're gonna do." Porter scratched his chin as he eyeballed at Malone.

"Yeah, I know." Malone reloaded the revolver.

"Be careful, man," Porter said.

"You know me," Malone answered quietly. "Slow down here on the bridge."

Malone wound down his window and carefully tossed the towel-wrapped knife into the Chicago River. He heard the splash and felt some more relief.

Malone then had Porter drive by Millennium Park. Together, they waited in the parking deck for State's Attorney Redford to leave his office. Once he did, they followed Redford north of town on the Dan Ryan Expressway to a large house on Keeler Avenue. They waited for Redford to go inside and get comfortable.

"You sure you know what you're doing?" Porter said.

"Yeah. I do," Malone said.

As Malone sat in the car, he thought of James and Ann and what the hell he would be doing in the future. He was just thankful he had some cash set aside.

"Okay, I'll be right back."

"You got it." Porter pulled up about a block down from Redford's and Malone got out of the car.

Slowly, he crept up to the house. Each step was painful, but he was focused on the task at hand. The garage door was still up and there was only the government-issued white Chevy, no other cars inside.

Redford seemed like the kind of guy who would have a security alarm or cameras, so Malone weighed his options. His thoughts were jumbled, and he was running on adrenaline and nothing else. Malone decided to go in through the open garage. He readied himself and carefully went inside. No alarm on the door. Good. He had to find Redford fast. He quickly scanned the kitchen. It was bright and modern and led right into the living room. No lights on. The place looked empty. Nothing out of the ordinary.

Going from the outside windows, he knew there were at least eight rooms in this house. Probably an office somewhere. Malone went up the stairs that led to a wide hallway with five doorways off of it. A guest bedroom was on the left. On the right was a bathroom, a child's bedroom with some bunkbeds, and a master suite was at the end of the hall. The hallway overlooked the living room, kitchen, and dining room.

The house was silent, except for the sound of some music playing quietly somewhere. Creeping silently, Malone found the office and saw Redford sitting behind a large wooden desk. He entered the office, revolver in hand, and Redford froze in fear.

Malone smelled alcohol. Grey Goose vodka. The same kind Redford drank when he was with underage prostitutes.

Redford started trembling. "I'm sorry, I'm sorry. Please don't. Don't."

"You're sorry, huh?" Malone aimed the revolver at Redford.

"Just so you know, I'm going to leak everything about you. Your wife, your kids, everyone's gonna know what a real piece of shit you were. I saw a few of those disgusting pictures on your phone."

"No—no—"

Malone pulled the trigger, shooting Redford in the side of the head. He fell from the chair and sprawled out on the floor. Malone saw something out of the corner of his eye and quickly turned around.

Redford's wife, Laurie, stood in the hallway by the office door. She screamed, her eyes glazed over in fear.

"I got no problem with you," Malone said quietly but firmly.

"What—what did he do?" Laurie's voice was trembling.

"Let's just say all the shit caught up to him."

Laurie's eyes moved down the hallway and she screamed again.

A Latino man with his arms covered in tattoos appeared, holding a handgun to Laurie's head. Malone didn't know his name, but recognized him from the Marriott.

Another Latino man in a black track suit appeared aiming a Glock at Malone. Malone immediately recognized him. Diego Gonzalez.

Malone shifted his eyes quickly from one gunman to another.

The tattooed man had a sly smile on his face as if he enjoyed was he was doing. "Drop it," the tattooed man said in a deep voice.

Malone studied him carefully. He recognized him from the shootout at the Marriott a few days ago. Malone didn't know his name. There was no hesitation in the man's voice, and he held the gun steady. This guy meant what he said.

"Okay. Okay. I'm putting my gun down, and you'll let her go?" Malone said.

"Mmm-hmm."

Malone dropped the revolver on the floor.

The tattooed man kept the gun aimed at Laurie.

"I dropped the gun, what the hell are you doing? Let her go!"

Another older Latino man in his fifties entered the room. He had on small, dark brown glasses, gray Armani suit, pressed white shirt, and silk navy tie. His posture was impeccable. Malone recognized him. The son of Ramon Garcia, José.

"I said let her go!" Malone screamed.

José picked up the revolver and studied Malone. A small smile came to his face. Not large enough to show any teeth, but enough to see José's lips had moved slightly. Then he shot Laurie in the head, and she tumbled to the floor.

"What the—why? Why'd you do that?" Malone blurted out.

"You know why, Sergeant Ryan Malone. She saw too much and knows too much," José replied.

"That's fucking bullshit."

"Sergeant Malone, you other concerns, such as your new assignment."

"Is that right?" Malone snapped.

"Yes, it is. You're working for us now," José replied.

"Tell me, who the fuck is *us*?"

The man sighed out loud. "I expect more from you, Ryan. I thought you were good at your job."

Malone sneered. "Kiss my ass."

"That's very rude, and you're already not in our good graces."

"What the hell are you talking about?"

"The money you stole from us a month ago, as well as from our associate here. Well, former associate. I also know about the money you've been keeping in your storage unit by Merchandise Mart."

It all immediately clicked in Malone's mind. The Latin Kings. They were working with Redford too. He was working with anyone and everyone.

"What the hell do you want from me?" Malone said.

"It's rather simple. When you're called, you're expected to answer that call," José handed Malone a phone. "If for some reason you don't answer, I'm confident you won't like the consequences of your actions."

Malone tightened his jaw. He wanted to shoot this prick in the head just like he did Redford. "Don't even think of hurting my family."

"Actually, you're not in the position to be making any demands. In fact, you don't look well. You need medical attention. Perhaps you can get a room with your son."

The words burned Malone's ears like acid. He had to fight the unbearable urge to charge at the men and strangle them both. Malone glared as he walked past the man in the suit and the tattooed man with wide eyes and his lip quivering.

"Don't worry, we'll take care of the bodies, as well as your gun."

The unknown Latino man picked up the revolver off of the floor.

"Talk to you soon, Ryan," José said with a crooked smile.

The words continued to sting in Malone's ears, and he was

so mad he could barely see straight. He wanted to strangle them both, but knew there was nothing he could do right now.

Malone headed toward the cruiser. Porter was slumped down in the driver's seat. Malone held his breath as he got closer and opened the door. Thankfully, he didn't see any blood. He finally took a deep breath and said, "Hey. Porter."

Porter jumped in the driver's seat.

"Shit. You okay, man?"

Malone ignored the question. "You see anything at all? Anyone pull up in a vehicle?" Malone was so tired now he could barely talk.

"No. I didn't. I guess I nodded off," Porter said with a shrug.

"Take me to Holy Cross. Use the siren and step on it."

Malone closed his eyes and wished this was all a bad dream.

"You gonna tell me what happened?"

"Later."

When the cruiser pulled up at Holy Cross, Malone moved as fast as he could, limping up to James' room. Ann was awake, and her eyes widened when she saw Malone hobble into the room. Malone's face was swollen face with dried blood on it and his hair was matted down flat with sweat.

"Hey."

"What the—are you okay?" Ann said.

"Yeah. Yeah. Anyone unusual come by? Anyone you don't know?"

"No, just some nurses. That's all."

"What happened to you? Why don't you sit down?"

"In a minute. Are you *sure* no one unusual came by here?"

No—no one."

"Good." Malone said.

"You really should get checked out by a doctor. Just go to the ER."

"I just need some rest," Malone said quietly.

"I have some good news," Ann said with a smile.

"Oh?" Malone's voice was getting quieter.

"The doctor says James is gonna be just fine, and we can leave tomorrow."

"Great," Malone's voice was now a whisper.

"Isn't it?" Ann replied. "Just such a relief."

Malone nodded his head slightly in agreement. "Yeah. That's really good."

Ann smiled. "I'll be right back. I'm going to go get you some ice from the cafeteria."

Malone nodded.

As soon as Ann left, Malone popped his last two painkillers in his mouth as he watched James sleep.

He then pulled out his phone and called Mitchell.

"Have you talked things over with your wife?"

"Yeah, I'll take the job."

"Okay. You'll be starting next week."

"All right. Thanks."

He stood by the window and saw his reflection. He ignored it, looking out at the Chicago skyline and the dark sky behind it.

"Hey, Dad," a voice said behind him. Malone quickly turned around, saw his son awake, and smiled.

THE STORY CONTINUES...

Yes, there's more to Ryan Malone's story. A lot more. Just visit www.authorjimwoods.net/free-stories/ to receive some free stories and keep up to date with what happens next.

www.ingramcontent.com/pod-product-compliance
Lightning Source LLC
Chambersburg PA
CBHW020123180726
47992CB00020B/1818